The Apocrypha of Eden

ISBN#
9781475027686

Cover art and layout design by Jill Quednow

Prologue

There is a source from which all things, all energy, all wisdom, and all time emanate. It is the pulsing wave that underlies the rhythmic sonance of the Universe (a word literally meaning "one song"). It is the force which allows a heart to beat, just as it is the source of the emotions and experiences which give meaning to the life that is sustained by the beating of that same heart. It is the kinetic potential for Creation or Destruction, of all that is, and all that ever could be.

It is all of these things, yet cannot truly nor accurately be contained or defined, for it flows freely and has no definition. Nonetheless, it seems the goal of many to harness, control, impose dogma, and ascribe a name unto this phenomena. And so, we name it God.

All that exists is not only the image of God, but is the essence of God itself. The spark that lights the heavens with the infinite expanse of stars, the mysteries of the life that exists within the darkest depths of the seas, the breeze that carries the tiniest speck of pollen to its destination, and the life and breath of each man all originate from one Source. When a man forgets or denies this truth, dividing himself from God, thinking God is something which dwells outside of him as something separate, it is the gravest error a man can make. When this occurs, and man acts in conflict against the Wisdom and Order which makes him one with God, it seems to be man's temptation to name demons or serpents culpable. In truth, the only demons that exist are the manifest design of man's own fears.

The names given to God have evolved and changed over time, as all things do, and so it has come to pass that the nature of God has been known differently by different people. Despite the conflicts, and even wars which stem from these differing names, in truth, the name is of no matter. What does matter is that there is a common thread that can either tie or separate humanity, and that thread is the longing to understand the meaning of God in their lives. This is evidenced by the fact that ever since the evolution of language, every tribe, every community, and every civilization that has existed has been drawn to pass down their beliefs and convictions to their young through storytelling. And thus, men cling to the traditions and stories of God they learned as children which bind them to their ancestors and give them a sense of kinship.

There is an immense power contained within these myths. This power can cause great pain and suffering if one clings too tightly to the details which distinguish one man's, or one community's, story from another. However, if these stories are received with openness and mindfulness of their common roots and purpose, they can offer insight and perspective to help man live with love, respect, and compassion for all that is around him; all that is God.

And if we are open in our minds and in our hearts, sometimes the story we thought we knew transforms into something quite different when cast in a new light.

One such story is that of a man named Adam and a woman called Eve. Their story is told herein as *The Apocrypha of Eden* ...

*Apocrypha = that which is hidden or unknown; mythical

Part I

Chapter 1

At the conception of Creation, God brought forth the immense force of gravity: the force which governs the cosmic dust, the random particles of matter, and the radiant waves of light and heat. Gravity could create and gravity could destroy. By harnessing this power, God unified matter and energy, and through this unity, He imposed Order and Law unto that which had been Entropy and Chaos. All was made to bend to the Will and the Wisdom of God, and by His hand, the Universe was born. God then amassed and arranged these charged particles of energy and matter to sculpt both Heaven and Earth.

God then formed a massive incandescent star, the Sun, whose continually burning fires of combustion would cast the illumination of day upon the face of the earth. This great star would hold the earth within its influence, nurturing it with its warmth and light, infusing its energy into all of the life which would dwell upon the earth. God commanded the separation of Shadow from Light, and set them into cycles in order to demonstrate that it is He who is the giver of Light, just as it is He who bears the power to cause Shadow and Darkness with the turning of the earth.

But it seemed that God could not bear the existence of utter darkness, and so He created the moon to cast its luminous glow upon the nighttime. Both the Dark and the Light would each serve their purpose. The sun's light would radiate life energy into all living things, and amid the darkness the waxing and waning of the moon would influence the ebb and flow of all the waters of the earth.

The stars which lit the expanse of the universe were born of the same original spark that is the Source of all things, and God set the stars among the umbra of the heavens in magnificent designs called constellations. The constellations would tell the stories of eons past, revealing the origins of the Universe. They would also serve as celestial guides, signs whereby the seasons, days, and years could be marked. The stars and planetary systems were composed into vast galaxies which span the heavens. And the entire Universe was made to vibrate with the sonorous pulsating rhythms of stellar explosions and the continual expanding and contracting breaths of the nebular clouds of dust.

The waters of the earth were then divided by great masses of rock and soil. There was land and sea. And unto the world, God brought forth the elements, the primal forces of nature and the organic components of life that combined and evolved to form all things. And from within the waters came the initial conception of animal life. Within the deepest abyss belies the mystery and ancestry of all the earth's descendants. And though the spark that ignites Life has its origin in the heavens, it is because the manifest forms of life on this earth were born first within these depths that water would forever be essential to the sustenance of all that would live upon the earth.

Next, God looked upon the terrain. He set into motion the courses of change that would cause certain of the creatures to be brought forth from the waters onto the land. In time, there came to dwell upon the soil every manner of beast, which would multiply and fill the earth with more of their kind. And as He had filled the seas and the land, so, too, did God fill the skies. He created creatures with wings to soar, as if to Heaven, to act as a sign of Life from above.

The land was adorned with thick, lush grasses and flowering bushes, all crafted delicately by God's masterful Hand. He created grains and fruited trees which would sustain all the creatures of the earth. These were made to grow bountiful and produce continually with no further labor and no need for tending, as the wind and the insects acted in perfect accord with God's Will to continue the cycle of life, transferring the pollen to generate fruit from the flower.

God had designed this world to evolve with the natural forces which He had inspired forth into motion, and so it was throughout the eras of time. All things continually shifted for age upon age of storms, floods, and destruction, and the face of the world was formed anew many times over. There were ages ruled by ice and cold that gave way to long periods of heat during which great forests were transformed into tundra, then to meadows, before growing into lush forests once again. Mountains pushed up from the bottoms of the oceans to reach far into the skies. Rushing waters cut through the mountains of rock, gouging out deep ravines through basalt and lime to resculpt the terrain. Great seas had dried up, shrinking to mere rivers and streams, only to swell with the rains and once again become vast oceans, leaving layers of sediment to tell the sagas of the earth's flux.

It came to pass that only certain of God's original creatures and vegetation had managed to live on, while a great number of others had died out. These had seen their time, and were simply unable to adapt, and no longer had a place amid the shifting environment. The ones that did continue to live on had developed the means to survive by evolving in accordance with the rise and fall of the waters and the coming together and moving apart of the lands. In being pliant to change and to the Will of God, they flourished.

Season followed season, and many millennia had come and gone when at last the time of waiting was over. God looked upon all He had done, and He saw that it was Good. For the land, the seas, the flora, and the fauna had finally reached the point of readiness. Now was the season for the next phase of Creation. The season of Man.

God gathered into His hands the clay of the earth, and combined it with water and particles of all of the elements of the universe, then sculpted it into the desired form. It was pure and beautiful. God then breathed Life Energy into the form and it became strong and vital. This was the first man, and God called him Adam.

Adam had difficulty understanding and accepting that the gifts of Creation had been given freely. He was afflicted with fear and uncertainty regarding his place in this world. He desired a path to follow in order to feel secure and to know that he was acting rightfully, so Adam petitioned God to give him guidance.

God loved Adam, and so He gave him that which he asked for. First, God set Eden apart from the rest of the world, to remain in its current state of perfection for all time. Because of the dependent nature he had shown, it did not seem that Adam would have the capacity to survive among the volatility of a changing world. Then, God created two Trees, rooted deeply and inextricably within the Gates of Eden, which man would believe to encompass two of the attributes of God. The first was the Knowledge of Good and Evil and the second was Eternal Life. Adam believed that to eat the Fruit of the Trees would be a trespass against God, causing man to be cursed and suffer a terrible death. Adam embraced the sense of security he derived from having this doctrine to adhere to, and he solemnly vowed to abide.

God then bestowed unto Adam dominion over the beasts and charged him with the naming of each. He told Adam that Eden was his home, and that he could roam freely, and that he would never know of hunger or thirst. God would always provide for his needs.

Adam spent many days giving names to each type of beast which dwelled in Eden, as well as to all of the varieties of plant life. There was beauty and harmony in all that surrounded him, yet Adam felt a deep desire he could not satisfy, a longing for something he did not yet have. He saw that the animals mated and communed with their own kind, and he wanted this for himself. Each day his loneliness deepened until finally, when he could bear it no more, he called out to Heaven, beseeching God to give him a companion.

God said "Adam, it is not right that you should remain alone in this way. It has always been part of My plan to provide you with a mate. I see now that it is time." God then returned to Heaven to wait for Adam to fall into slumber, for it was then that He would form a companion for him.

God's heart spoke to Him regarding the consideration needed to create a woman which would best befit Adam. God recognized that Adam had been forged reflecting only the masculine nature of His own image. God saw that in this, Adam may be deficient in the qualities that would open him to lightness and joy. Adam was strong and firm, but did not know empathy, nor how to bend or yield. He was constant and steadfast, like the clay from which he was molded. He had reason, but lacked intuition and creativity. He was faithful to his Creator, but did not possess the qualities of independence and autonomy, needing doctrines and dogma to live by. Without a being created from the strongest of feminine attributes, there would be no harmony or balance among humankind.

As Adam lie within a deep sleep, God came to him. God removed bone and marrow from Adam's body and proclaimed: "She shall be created from him and thus they will be intrinsically connected. She will belong to him and they will be as one flesh." Just as with Adam's creation, the woman's form was infused with the energy which emanates from the original Source of light and heat that is the genesis of all things. So too, were integrated all of the elements that had been gathered when Adam was formed, though in varying measure. As Adam was mainly constituted from the clay and minerals of the earth, God determined that his mate would possess more of the flow and rhythm of the waters, and her flesh would be soft and yielding. When God had completed the sculpting of the female's body, He rested it gently upon the ground.

It was time for the Breath of Life to be given, to meet and merge with the fire that drives the essence of femininity. When the Breath of Life came into contact with this fire, there was a violent combustion...

Chapter 2

One moment, there is stillness, lightness, a gentle hush... Then suddenly a caustic burning as oxygen is sucked violently and rapidly into lungs, forcing them to expand painfully. Desperate gasps follow as thoracic muscles and pleura repeatedly dilate and contract in their struggle to pull in more and more air. Eyes struggle to blink open against the assaulting, stinging glare of sunlight. Immediately they fill with tears which spill over into salty streams that streak downward and fall upon the earth. The entire form convulses upon the ground, overwhelmed by the abrupt thrust of atoms and particles into anatomical systems of function, linked together to form one being; a being instantly required to take on environmental stimuli and adapt to life without the benefit of gestation.

*   *   *

This was the moment of her "birth". She lay upon the soft grass, struggling with each breath to fill her lungs with air while her muscles continued to twitch and jerk intermittently, though slowly she began to gain some control. The pain in her eyes gradually subsided, and along with this the unfocused appearance of light and dark began to separate into the forms of discernable shapes and images, though all of these were unknown to her. Looking up from where she lay, she perceived what she would come to know as "green". Beyond that, what appeared to be unending "blue". She could see creatures moving far above her. Some were soaring high in that vast blueness, and some were gliding swiftly from green to green. Melodic sounds emanated from them, and these sounds seemed to act upon her in a way that helped slow her breathing, and further quieted the spasms of her muscles. She felt an urge to move, and slowly sat up. There came an immediate throbbing pressure behind her eyes, and her head was overwhelmed with a heavy dizziness, forcing her to remain where she was, immobile on the ground. She felt restricted and weighed down by her body. Everything she perceived caused her confusion, and she wanted an answer. She wanted many answers. She knew somehow that being in this place, whatever it was, was something new that she had not experienced before, and she felt sure that she had been part of some other state of existence before awakening to this form. She did not know why or how she had come to be there, and she was both frightened and agitated by her lack of understanding. Filled with the fear of uncertainty, she began trembling as her breath once again became uneven and shallow. Fresh tears streamed down her face as her heart beat fiercely against the wall of her ribcage. Despair and dread filled her with a longing to return to whatever or wherever she had originated from. She gave in to these feelings and began to weep without control; hyperventilating, choking and gasping.

Then, a voice that seemed to speak from somewhere within her commanded her to stop and to breathe. She thought the voice to be her own, yet was not entirely certain, though it mattered not. All that mattered was that it was right. She knew that she had to stop her tears and focus her energy instead on discovering what was happening to her. With great effort, she exerted control over her fear and managed to regain some semblance of calmness and found herself once again driven by her desire for answers. In her renewed determination, she had forgotten her dizziness and unsteadiness, and stood up abruptly. All at once the colors above and around her began to whirl and spin, blending together sickeningly, and legs that had never before borne weight lost their fight against the influence of gravity as they tremored violently and folded beneath her, bringing her crashing to the ground, unconscious.

Chapter 3

It was mostly a vision of remembrance, and it began with a sense of warmth and lightness. The feeling originated from somewhere deep within, then spread out of her in waves, becoming infinite and expansive. There was a sense of all things being One, with a common thread that was woven throughout to create a unified divinity. It was bliss. Then, by the will of some unknown Hand, there occurred a massive division of this Oneness, followed by an abrupt fusing of elements into a new union that caused a violent flare, and the bliss was shattered. After moments of darkness, she experienced, within the dream, a gentle wind which first moved past her, then through her, and finally, this air was her. It became her very breath. It whispered softly within her heart, and she felt at peace...

Her peace was suddenly broken as she was startled into consciousness by the sudden awareness of a presence hovering directly over her. When her eyes opened she saw a being similar to herself. She felt unnerved, even threatened, by his closeness. All she could do was lie there, waiting motionless and quiet, in anticipation of what would happen. Then, he spoke...

"I am Adam, son of God. You are the woman whom God has provided in order to be my companion throughout my days. We are the only two of our kind, though God has commanded us to consummate and perpetuate mankind, and thus His flock shall grow.

"It is upon me to teach you the story of Creation and of the Creator. I will show to you the bounty He hath bestowed within this place of dwelling, called Eden. I will teach to you the names of all living things, for it was I who was entrusted by God to give their names unto them."

"Most importantly, I will instruct you in the canons of our God. For it is our duty to follow the laws which the Creator has set forth, and to live in deference to His power and wisdom. As we both must obey God, so too must you obey me, for God has forged your flesh from my own, and ever shall you cleave unto me."

She could barely absorb the things he was saying. Though she was somehow able to understand his words, she had no reference from which to give meaning to much of it. She was a stranger in this place, and she felt an overwhelming empty loneliness for something she was unable to grasp, but had felt close to returning to within her dream. She realized that it was now her reality to be in this body and to live upon this earth. This man before her said she was to be his companion and comply with his bidding. She felt she had little choice, as he seemed to know things of which she knew nothing. He even seemed to know who she was, and could possibly give her the answers that would help her understand her existence here.

When he had stopped talking, Adam offered his hand to help her rise up. She found standing to be easier this time, feeling a greater sense of stability which came not only from the physical support he gave her, but also from the firm strength within his touch. And though she had been frightened by him at first, being close to him now calmed her and made her feel safe.

He continued to hold onto her while her body and senses adapted to being upright. The landscape wavered and swayed before her, but no longer appeared to spin, nor did it cause the same sickening within her as it had the last time she tried to stand. There was a gradual balancing within her ears and in the movements of her eyes. After gently moving and stretching her limbs to get a better sense of her body, she felt able to attempt walking. Her steps at first were very slow and cautious, and as she continued to walk, her legs would often begin to tremble and she frequently stumbled. She needed to ask Adam to stop and allow her to rest many times. He always paused for as long as she needed, though she could tell he was eager to continue on.

He said, "There is so much for you to behold in Eden. It is the time of day in which the beasts gather to drink and cool themselves by the water. Your own thirst must be great."

As Adam spoke, her attention was drawn to the fact that her mouth had indeed become very dry. Too dry even to answer him. All she could do was nod her head in agreement. They began walking again, and after a time, he told her they were near.

As they passed through the edge of the dense trees, her eyes beheld a sight that made her heart beat fast with excitement and wonder. The entire field of her vision was filled with the multitudes of beautiful creatures gathered along the bank of the river. As she took in the amazing sight, her thirst was temporarily forgotten. The diversity of size, texture, form, and color was punctuated by the apparent peace in which they dwelled there together. Despite the tranquility of the scene, she felt hesitant in proceeding any further. She looked to Adam for reassurance. He seemed to understand, and said:

"There is nothing to fear. Man is meant to live in harmony with all of Creation. There is an inherent respect and order among all living things. That is Nature. Let us go and drink alongside the animals."

They walked forth to the water's edge and knelt down. The woman was about to bow down low to drink as she had seen the beasts do, but then Adam cupped his hands together and dipped them into the river. He brought the handful of liquid to her lips. She opened her mouth and closed her eyes. A taste of cool sweetness hit her tongue. As it passed down her throat and into her body, she began to feel herself become somehow lighter, and a new sense of energy came upon her. She opened her eyes and once more beheld the sight of the high and dense forest which grew on both sides of the great river. She looked above to the vast and infinite blue and saw the graceful creatures which could glide upon the wind. She regarded again the great variety of beasts gathered, like her, at this place where the water rushes forth to nourish, cool, and give relief from thirst and weariness. With her own exhaustion and fears seemingly washed away by the sweet drink, it was with new, clear eyes that she now contemplated all of these things. She found that she no longer felt she was a stranger in this place, and it was as though she could sense the Hand of her own creation in the creation of all of these wondrously beautiful living things.

When she and Adam had both drank as much as their bellies could hold, Adam arose and once again offered his hand to her. He said, "As I have told you, God has charged me with the naming of the animals. Come, and I will teach you what each is called."

As they came upon each type of beast, Adam told her its name, and bade it to move in its own manner before her so that she could see the individual qualities of each. Their ways of movement were quite varied and there was an exquisite diversity in the patterns and textures of their skins. Some were spotted or striped, some were covered in thick, coarse coats, and some had smooth, fine hair that shone sleekly in the sun. Some had no hair, but instead scales, feathers, or other various forms of covering upon them. She touched her hands to each of them, and found an extreme pleasure in the different sensations she experienced. The animals, too, seemed to enjoy the feeling of being touched. The woman was delighted when she learned that the sounds they made were as varied as their appearances. Some produced deep sounds with a growling quality. The ones which could spread their wings and fly, those that Adam called birds, sang out in the sweet, melodic songs she had heard upon her first awakening. And there were many indescribable sounds, such as those that came from the elephants and the frogs. Their sounds caused her to laugh with delight.

All of the creatures were magnificent to behold, and her initial sense of wonder only increased as she became more acquainted with each. She noticed the way each of them seemed to regard her, taking in the way she moved and listening to the sounds she made as well. She turned toward Adam.

"It fills me with a deep joy to be able to know creatures such as these. Though they are all so different from you and me, I feel there is a connection between us."

As she said this, a sudden spark came into Adam's eyes and he replied, "There is another creature I have yet to show you. Let us go deep within the trees to find them."

She followed him back toward the forest, walking until at last they came upon a grassy area within a ring of trees where great vines hung down all around them from the thick overhanging canopy above. The leaves occluded much of the sky, yet the sun that did seep in came through in beautiful rays that cut through small gaps in the foliage at various points, creating long, glistening beams of gold that originated in the heavens and reached down to touch upon the forest floor. Small insects and particles of pollen were illuminated in the dewy air, making them dance and sparkle within the streams of sunlight. The woman took the vision in, enchanted by the profound beauty of it all, barely daring to breathe, lest she disturb the perfection she perceived all around her.

Adam bid her to remain quiet and watch. They both stood in silence for a long while, and as she waited her anxiety grew along with her curiosity, and it became increasingly difficult to remain still. Then at last, she heard something. It began as a rustling of the leaves and some unknown call that echoed through the trees. Soon more calls filled the air, seeming to emanate from all directions, until suddenly, from somewhere in her periphery, a large dark form swung down in front of her. It swooped directly past her and then off to the other side, making a noise that seemed to be both screeching and laughing at the same time. She turned toward Adam in astonishment and was about to ask what it was, but before she could speak several more of the creatures came swinging down all around them. She watched as they moved adeptly among the branches and vines. Several times she was certain that two of them were about to collide, or that one was going to fall, and she would gasp out loud. This caused Adam to look at her, and then both of them would laugh at her unfounded reaction, for the creatures moved with an effortless grace and precision, never falling, and never missing their mark. The sounds of the creature's laughter and hooting continued, and it was obvious that this was only play to them.

After a while, some of them ventured off to find new vines and trees to swing and play among, but a few came nearer to where Adam and the woman sat.

Adam said, "These are but one species of a family of creatures I have termed 'apes'."

One of the apes walked directly toward her, and stood with her face close to the woman's. The light feeling of joy and amusement left her, replaced by a solemn, silent awe. She felt a familiar sense of recognition pass between them. Adam had said that he and she were the only two of their kind, the only humans, and though she still believed his words to be true, it was very apparent to her that these beings were somehow set apart from the other beasts, and could not be regarded quite the same.

The ape raised one of her hands and, instinctually, the woman did the same. With their palms touching, the paralleled structure of their hands was pronounced and undeniable. As they looked upon each other it was as though their eyes were searching within the eyes of the other for some revelation. She perceived an overwhelming sense of a forgotten past in the creature's eyes. They appeared ancient and wise, and conveyed what the woman thought to be a quality of sadness or loss. She wondered at what it was that those eyes had seen, and what secrets they held. She knew that she was witnessing something significant, but at the same time could not help but feel that she was missing something of an even deeper meaning and importance, something just beyond her grasp. It was as if there was a space within each of them that lie unfulfilled that this creature could somehow see, but she could not. Lost in the gaze and in her own thoughts, the woman was startled as the ape reached out to her and gently wiped away a tear she hadn't even realized was falling down her cheek. The moment was suddenly over as the ape abruptly turned away, let out another of its laughing, hooting sounds, and swung away on one of the vines, disappearing back into the trees. She tried to take pause to absorb what had just happened and to try to make sense of it, but found that she could not. So she turned to Adam instead, hoping for clarity.

He said, "I understand your tears, as well as the questions which lie behind them, for these same feelings have often come upon me when I regard the face of one of them, seeing into their eyes, so much like our own. I feel there is a mystery or secret that I cannot know." Adam's body then became very tense and his voice changed, bearing a peculiar harshness tinged with anguished resignation as he continued, "God hath determined that it be thus, however, and it is not for you, nor I, to question His ways. Whatever answers He has not seen fit to reveal to me, I shall not seek to know."

She was confused and a little frightened by the change in him, and though she could not comprehend the reason he spoke to her in this manner, she did not undertake to ask him to explain further. Adam seemed to calm down when it was evident that she would not press him to say more, and soon he regained his usual tone as if it had not happened. Her concern over his reaction eventually subsided as she had grown both weary and hungry and did not have the energy to consider it further.

Adam picked fruit from the trees and told her what each one was called. Everything he offered to her tasted sweet and gave her a feeling of pleasure and contentment. After eating, they both lay down upon the bed of palm leaves Adam had spread out on the warm earth for them.

Adam had fallen asleep almost as soon as he had stretched out upon the ground, but as the woman looked up into the night sky, her head teemed with endless questions. She desired to know more about everything. More about herself, about Adam, the animals, the plants, the sky....especially the sky. As she continued to gaze upward, she wondered at its mysteries. It had been so clear and bright during the day, but now had grown so changed with the coming of the darkness. She wondered how far that blackness continued on behind all of those pulsating points of light and the one shining crescent hanging high in the expanse above her. Adam had called these things the stars and the moon. Looking at them stirred something deep within her. It was a numinous sense of presence and of limitlessness. It reminded her of something she had felt in her vision when she had fallen unconscious, something that seemed a part of a beautiful but elusive mystery. She wanted to know and to understand what they were, how they came to be, and if they meant something. She wondered where the large, fiery star that shone in the daytime sky had gone to. Adam had called it the Sun. And she wanted to know more about the God Adam had spoken of, too. She wished to understand all of these things, and so much more. Everything held such splendor and wonder for her, she was nearly overwhelmed by her eagerness to take it all in. As she lie there, endless thoughts and questions spun around in her mind. And as the night wore on, they continued spinning, gradually spiraling farther and farther away, becoming cloudy and obscured by exhaustion, until at last they gently faded out of the reach of consciousness. She had no choice but to let all of her questions go as sleep overtook her.

Chapter 4

It felt as though she had spent the entire night encompassed in that same vision which seemed to exist somewhere so far away and so different. When she had mentioned her unconscious vision the day before to Adam, he had explained to her that these visions during sleep were called dreams. This one seemed so real and felt like a memory, but nothing like the way she could remember all of the things that had happened the day before, like meeting Adam, seeing the apes, drinking the water, or touching the animals. There was nothing that was like any of those experiences in her dream. Instead there was heat, and fire, and particles enmeshed in a continual cycle of colliding and bursting, condensing and collapsing in powerful, almost violent blasts of energy that were both beautiful and frightening in their intensity. There was also an omnipresent unifying wave she could sense that caused these particles, and even the space they occupied, to expand and contract with a cadence and rhythm like that of a breath.

Her dream gradually faded and consciousness descended upon her more gently this day, quite unlike either of her previous two awakenings, which had been abrupt and unsettling. When she opened her eyes and beheld the brilliantly illuminated Garden she felt a tangible live energy which emanated from all things around her that filled the atmosphere. She realized that perhaps this energy, too, was like the ever present rhythm she had experienced in her dream. She breathed in deeply, then let out a soft, contented sigh as the wind blew past her, carrying on it both the songs of the birds and the fragrant aromas of the waking flowers.

She looked around for Adam and saw him walking toward her, his hands filled with many kinds of fruits. Seeing him caused her to smile. There was a pleasant, warm feeling in watching him come to her, bringing her food. He returned her smile, and asked:

"Are you rested from your sleep?"

"Yes, and I am filled with eagerness to learn all that you can teach me. I want to understand all of this. I feel the questions will overflow and consume me if not soon met with answers."

Laughing, Adam replied, "You must be patient, and I will tell you of all things which have been revealed to me by God. But first, let us eat of these sweet fruits, which He has provided to nourish and satisfy our needs. We must always remember that it is He who bestows all gifts unto us, and He who has given us life itself."

Though she found it difficult, she suppressed her questions while they ate. When at last they both had finished, Adam stood up and spoke:

"Come, we shall walk throughout the Garden, and I will give you the answers to all that you ask."

After the build-up that resulted from so much restraint, she was momentarily struck mute; her words caught all together her throat. She looked around her, trying to decide where to begin. There was so much, and she wanted to know all of it. At last she took in a deep, slow breath, found her voice, and the questions burst forth from her in rapid succession.

Adam spent the day telling her more about the beasts, the trees, flowers, roots, and herbs. He taught to her the names of the celestial bodies, drawing their outlined forms upon the dirt to illustrate them while explaining their movements in the sky, and showed her how to mark time by their positions. The woman learned of the cycles of dark and light, which cause night and day. She learned the words that describe colors, and sounds, and textures.

As Adam patiently continued to show new things to her, giving explanations and answering question upon question she asked of him, the woman could sense that he enjoyed the opportunity to speak to her of these things with such knowing. She herself experienced a deep pleasure from listening to him and learning from him.

Upon looking up, she noticed how the burning star, the sun, had traversed and ascended the sky, reaching its highest point. She now understood that this indicated a certain passing of time, and half of the day's light had gone by. She and Adam agreed that it was again time to eat and drink. They returned to the river, which Adam had said was the source of the four great rivers which flowed outside the gates of Eden, called the Pishon, Gihon, Tigris, and Euphrates. Once more the river's shores were lined with multitudes of creatures pacifying their thirst at the water's edge and grazing among the tall grasses. She sat and watched them as she and Adam ate the sweet dates and almonds that they had gathered along the way.

After eating and drinking as much as they could, they lay back on the soft grass. The woman closed her eyes and felt her skin absorb the sun's radiance and warmth into her body. She felt as if the sun had become a part of her, transferring its energy throughout her being. A gentle wind then moved across her flesh. She breathed it into her lungs, and it, too, merged with her body. Her exhale was then carried off with the next breeze, to blend with the essence of some plant or animal. Her awareness had undergone a subtle shift. No longer did she feel the barrier of flesh or even space between the elements of her own existence and that of all other life. There was an attunement of every cell, every particle, which created an organic unity between her being and all that surrounded her. All things were as one, and she *was* the very essence of the air, the water, the grass and the flowering buds.

Being fully absorbed in that beautiful, deep, and unexplainable awareness was sadly ephemeral, and the depth of her revelation faded as she sensed Adam stirring next to her. It then seemed just beyond her grasp, like the feelings she wished she could hold onto within her dreams. The sensation was nearly the same; it was the feeling of returning to a oneness, a sort of remembrance of a glorious connection of all things, stemming from a sense of a common origin where the boundaries of matter, or even the concept of boundaries, did not exist. Although, she found upon opening her eyes and regaining focus of her more tangible surroundings that the world did not allow for her to feel any great disappointment. All that she could see, smell, touch, and taste in the Garden caused a profound sense of joyful gratitude, and she derived an immense pleasure in experiencing this world through the perceptions of her flesh.

She turned to look at Adam, lying beside her. She could tell by his deep, rhythmic breathing that he was still in a sound sleep. She watched him for a long while and noticed that even though the usual tension held in his face and body appeared more relaxed, there remained a striking quality of solidity and firmness about him. She suddenly had the impression that Adam seemed composed of the same substance of the firm earth beneath him. There was a strength and security in this which she was drawn to. Yet, she also perceived a limitation within the presence of too much of these qualities. She then realized that he did not always see or experience certain things the same way that she did. She wondered if this would include the way that she had just felt the intrinsic connectedness between herself and all of Creation. The thought that he might not perceive these same things brought an aching within her chest that she had not known before. It was a sad longing to be able to share the beauty of what she had experienced with him.

"Both of us being the same, being human," she thought, "shouldn't we both have the capacity to experience what transcends this flesh?" While she was considering this, Adam awoke. He stood and stretched. She wanted to talk to him about it, to see if he could perhaps comprehend what she had perceived, but he spoke first.

"There is something that I must show you right now."

"What is it?"

He smiled widely and said, "How to be a fish!"

He ran toward the water and dove into it, disappearing from her sight. His actions startled her, making her forget entirely what had been on her mind. She began to grow anxious after many moments had passed and he did not re-appear. Her eyes scanned the water for some indication of where he was, but even the ripples caused by his submersion had disappeared. She called out his name several times, her voice growing more tremulous and urgent with panic each time she repeated it. She ran up and down along the shore. "Where could he be? Is he ok?" These thoughts tormented her as she continued to call out his name again and again. Looking down the river a short distance, she noticed bubbles rising to the surface. And suddenly there he was, head and shoulders emerging from the water. She watched as he paddled his arms and seemed to be kicking his legs and feet in a manner that propelled him forward. He came to the shore where she stood. He pulled himself up beside her on the grass and laughed.

"My, what a somber expression you wear."

Her heart pounded fiercely, and her face had become hot and flushed. She had been so worried, thinking that she had somehow lost him, and now he laughed at her concern and confusion. But just as she was about to admonish him for his actions, he laid his hands gently upon her shoulders, and spoke to her in a low, soothing voice.

"I did not mean to frighten you. I had hoped to make you laugh. You must come with me into the water and experience it for yourself. I think you will enjoy it. However, you must refrain from trying to take in any breath when you are below the water. The whole time I was under, I did not breathe. Do you think you can do that?"

Though his voice and his touch had quelled her fury and anxiety, her own voice still trembled a little when she answered him.

"I know I can, for I also did not breathe the whole time you were under the water and I could not see you."

She wasn't sure why, but this caused them both to suddenly burst out in laughter. Perhaps it was from the relief and release of worry: her worry about losing him, and Adam's worry about her being angry with him.

She sat down at the water's edge, and Adam jumped back into the river. He reached out his hands and took her by the waist, lifted her gently up off the ground, and then lowered her into the water next to him.

Any apprehension she had felt was completely dissolved away the moment she became immersed within this new realm. She remembered how, with her first drink of water, a lightness and a sense of renewal had come upon her. This was the same feeling, but intensified to such magnitude that it filled her entire being, making each cell feel weightless and buoyant. She dove down deeper within the river. There was a fluid rhythm both in and around her. She felt herself carried by this rhythm but not controlled by it. Her motions were free and flowing. The water and the woman acted as forces upon each other, but without inflicting will or resistance. Despite all of the wonders she had witnessed, she could not have imagined that a place such as this could exist. A hidden world, that was all at once serene and tranquil, yet abundant with the divine spark of life's energy. She came upon an underwater forest of tall, willowy plants, rooted from the bottom of the river. They swayed with the flow of the undercurrent. Their undulating motion was mesmerizing and hypnotic. She was held enchanted as she watched the fish that darted back and forth, weaving their way through the billowing stalks.

She noticed how the light from the sun bent as it penetrated the surface of the water, casting its illumination differently than it did upon the land. It caused her eyes to perceive everything, including her own limbs, as if part of a hazy, mystical reminiscence of a dream.

All sounds seemed as echoes from far away, yet she could also hear echoes from within; the sounds of her own heartbeat, and of her blood, pulsing strongly throughout her body. These were the sounds of her own strength and vitality, and she became aware of the potency of her own life force. Within this watery realm, it seemed that she was no longer bound by the same laws of physical motion, sensory perception, or even weight as upon the land. Yet, she was still limited by her need to breathe, and her lungs were beginning to burn. She ascended and breached the surface of the water. The act of forcefully drawing air into her lungs caused her to briefly recall the feeling of her first gasp for breath, though without the intense panic or struggle of those initial moments of life.

As she had been rapt in this experience, Adam had been watching her through the surface of the water. Apparently she had been oblivious to anything else for a long span of time while she was below, for Adam said:

"Did you forget me? I have been trying to get you to swim with me, but you move in and out of the depths so fast, and maneuver beneath the water with such swiftness and ease, that all I could do was watch in wonder. It appears as if you originated from the waters." He laughed, and added, "Perhaps you are truly a fish, or possibly a water serpent!"

She laughed too, but she considered these words of his regarding her origin. His notion of her being of the waters seemed remarkably similar to her own observations just a short time earlier regarding Adam's essence being of the minerals and soil of the earth. Despite his making light of it, it occurred to her that there was perhaps a deep truth within what they both had witnessed in each other that caused her to wonder, but she did not say any of this aloud to Adam, for she feared he would not understand or that he would tell her that she was wrong.

She let this thought pass, and together they splashed and played in the river until the sun began its descent in the sky. Some of the animals had stood by and watched their carefree antics for a while, but now they had gone off, likely to settle down for sleep.

They got out of the water to seek their own rest and to find food. Though it had become cooler with the setting of the sun, the air was still warm enough to dry their skin and hair by the time they had gathered and eaten their fruits. Once again, Adam set down leaves of palm for them to sleep upon. They lay down together, both feeling a happy, satisfied kind of exhaustion from all they had done that day. The woman could not find the words to express to Adam the depth of how thankful she was for all that he had shown to her and shared with her. Instead of words, she put her hand in his, hoping that somehow her touch could convey how she felt. She did not let go the entire night.

They spent day after day in this same way, and each night her head was filled with images and dreams. Most often, the dreams had that same cosmic essence of a primary Source, where light and heat were continually engaged in a dance of merging together and splitting apart. It was always spectacularly intense and beautiful. And with each dawning of the sun came new wonders and magnificent things for her to discover. Adam continued to teach her about their world, expanding on the lessons of the previous days. He seemed to know so much about everything in Eden. She eagerly drank in all that he told her, and always yearned for more. The more she learned, the more she began to see new connections between things, such as the time Adam was explaining the way the plants absorb the light of the sun, and use it to make their own nourishment. She was filled with delight as she realized that when they ate the fruit of the plants, in essence, they were taking in the energy of the sun, and its radiance was then inside them. Adam told her that he had never seen it that way before, but that what she said seemed true.

Each day they returned to the river near the time when the sun had reached its zenith in the sky. They would run, jump, climb, swim and play until, overcome by sweet exhaustion, they would fall asleep by the shore, lulled by the sound of the water's movement and the warmth of the soft, grassy earth. All was perfect. Calm. Placid.

Then came a day that was different. Adam was much quieter than usual. He was less playful, more distant and serene, and he had remained so throughout the day. Though she did not understand the reason for this, the woman waited patiently for him to talk to her. Finally, in the evening, before lying down to sleep, he said to her:

"Throughout these days, there have been many lessons, but none as important as what I will teach to you tomorrow. You have spent much time learning of Creation. Tomorrow you shall learn of the Creator."

There was a grave tone in his voice. It was that same tone that he always seemed to acquire whenever he spoke of his God. It disturbed and unsettled her, and began to give rise to a fear in meeting what tomorrow's lesson may hold.

She decided, however, to push this thought aside and keep her silence regarding any apprehensions. She had enjoyed all of her days thus far with Adam, so why should she fear that tomorrow would be so different? She let go of her worries and closed her eyes, letting the joyful images of them playing in the river wash over her and carry her into sleep.

Chapter 5

The sun arose, dispersing the nighttime darkness and lifting the veil of sleep from her eyes. Adam was already up, and appeared to have been waiting for her to awaken and eat with him. He looked to have been up since long before the dawn, and she realized that he must have gathered their food while it was still dark.

He wore a stern expression, and hardly seemed to acknowledge her as she sat down beside him. They ate together in silence. She did not feel right interrupting the thoughts that seemed to be keeping him so far away. It was not until their meal was finished that he spoke.

"I feel such a great importance regarding the things you will learn this day. There is a weight upon me to convey the words of our Lord unto you. I must try to do justice to the glory of God."

There remained the same unsettling quality in his tone she had heard the day before. It carried a peculiar mix of fear and gravity and made him seem deeply pained. She wanted to give him assurance, so she looked upon him warmly and spoke gently to him.

"You have taught me so many things with great clarity and knowledge. I will listen to your teachings attentively, and learn from you as I always have."

Adam heaved a heavy sigh of resolve and said, "Then let us go to the place of this lesson." He stood and reached his hand down to her. She took it and rose up, following Adam as he led the way.

They walked until they had come upon a grove of fruited trees. Adam chose one, then bade her to sit with him beneath its shade.

He began by telling her the story of God, recounting that He was the Creator of all: Earth, Heaven, the beasts, the trees, the waters, the wind, and the two of them. Adam then told her that man was the reason for which all else was created.

These last words confused her, and she felt compelled to interrupt him.

"Wait," she said, "there is so much beauty in all things which live within the Garden. Nature has an essence of purity and a rhythm that we are a part of, but without us, it would not be less wondrous. Do you really think that the birds fly and the fish swim just for you? It seems somehow wrong to think this way."

She saw his jaw tighten at her words. But then he took a deep breath and seemed to relax as he started speaking again.

"Of course, you do not realize your error, for you do not yet understand. It is necessary that you listen to all that I have to tell you. I am sure you will come to see what I mean, and you will know that what I say is not to be questioned."

Adam continued on, and she told herself to be patient, and that perhaps it was simply a matter of her not quite understanding his meaning. She would let him speak without further interruption, and perhaps after she had heard all he had to say it would make greater sense to her.

He told her again of his own first days in Eden, when God revealed to him the wonders of His Creation, and how God had given unto him dominion of all the beasts, and had charged him with naming all of the creatures and caring for them.

"This task occupied me for a great time, and I found much joy in the beauty of the Garden, and in the companionship of the animals, just as I see you have. But there came a day that I realized my singularity among the other creatures. The animals often dwell in groups of their same likeness, and they pair together, but I had no other like me. In His greatness, God listened to my prayers, and knew of my loneliness. He told me that I would be given a companion with whom I could dwell."

"He then caused me to fall into a deep sleep, during which time He culled flesh from my body. From this foundation, His Hand sculpted you into the form of woman. You are from my very substance, and thus you shall always cling unto me, and adhere to my will and intentions, and to the Will of God. You shall honor me as your husband, and I shall be sovereign over you. You are to be my mate and do my bidding to fulfill our duty to God to populate the earth, and in this way, His flock shall grow."

Adam paused, and there was silence between them. She found herself unable to move, or speak, or even to take in a regular breath. Only shallow sips of air were able to pass through the tightening within her throat. She felt herself engulfed by the sudden weight of the atmosphere, compressing her from every direction, while her ears were filled with a high pitched ringing that seemed to come from within her own head, accompanied by the echoes of the words he had spoken, 'I shall be sovereign over you', 'adhere to my will' and 'do my bidding'. She then recalled that Adam had told her something like this the very first time they met. She had paid little attention that day, as she was disoriented, confused, and had such trouble in simply standing. Now, however, his words struck hard at her. How was it possible that he could regard her in this way?

Could Adam truly feel that he ruled over her, over the animals, and even over all of nature? Did he honestly believe that a god had created not only her, but everything that exists, simply for Adam to use as he pleased? She was so hurt by this betrayal that she didn't know what to do or say. She could not even bring herself to look at him.

They sat within a shroud of dismal silence for a long while. When her head had finally begun to clear, she turned her gaze back upon Adam. His words had torn through her, and they were a harsh treason against her heart. All that she had perceived regarding their friendship could not co-exist with the words he had just spoken. She could feel a great chasm growing between them, and it seemed to widen with each silent moment that passed. Her stomach ached, and she wanted to run. She wanted to be far away from this stranger before her, this man whom she had known as her friend and as her teacher. As she moved to stand up and leave his presence, he grasped her wrist to stop her and said:

"Wait, you cannot leave now. That was only a part of what you need to know. There is more that I must tell you if you are to live by the canons of our Lord."

His words were nearly beyond belief to her. Was it possible that he could not see how he had affected her and caused her sorrow? Or could it be that he was simply not concerned with her feelings? She said nothing, however. She sat down again without protest, deciding to hear him out in full, though his words may further estrange her heart from him. His voice broke through her silent thoughts.

"Our God is a God of love. And because He loves us, He wants to keep us safe from things unknown to us. He gave us Eden, where all of our needs are satisfied, and we shall never know wanting or hunger. Outside the gates of Eden, however, the world continues to change and shift. The forces of nature continue to act upon the waters and the land. There is perhaps a wild kind of beauty out there, for it is still part of God's creation, but there are great storms that ravage the terrain. And there are many dangers and evils of which we are unaware. In Eden, however, God has brought Nature to a level of placidity. It is unchanging."

Adam continued, "Here, we can live without concerning ourselves with choices or conflict. Save for one choice. Look now upon the tree under which we are sitting. On first sight it may appear to you to be as all other trees of its kind. But hear this clearly: you must heed the Law of God and never eat the Fruit of this Tree, for it is the Tree of Knowledge. To eat from it is to become gnostic of Good and Evil. It is not for us, as humans, to know of these things, for this Knowledge is a Godly attribute. The Tree is a sign of God's supremacy over us, as well as a way for us to evince our complete piety and devotion to His Will. We must not succumb to the temptation of the Fruit, for we would lose our innocence through this act. This transgression would bring great pain, agony, and ultimately, death. By abstaining from the fruit of the Tree, we may live here throughout our days, without care or need. Free from the responsibilities of knowledge and choice."

Chapter 6

She stood up slowly and walked away. It was all she could do. Her head felt numb, leaving her incapable of even beginning to attempt to sort it all out. She simply kept walking: walking as if she thought she could walk away from this pain, away from her feelings of loss and betrayal. But the pain burned from within her, and there was nowhere she could go to truly escape it. She was unaware of what direction she was moving. Unaware of anything around her.

She continued on, and the remainder of the day slipped by unnoticed until it finally began to grow dark. She found a soft patch of grass beneath a small date palm, and there she lay herself down. She felt listless and weak, and vaguely realized that she had not eaten anything since daybreak, but it did not matter. She had no desire for food. Her stomach was filled with a sour sickness and a gripping tension, leaving no room for anything else. She remembered how, on so many days, she had awoken to the sight of Adam walking toward her after having gathered food for them. She had always felt such joy at the sight of him. That joy was now so far from her heart, seeming to her as if it were really only a vague memory. A memory which now felt distorted and false.

Her head began to hurt and she felt an intense throbbing behind her eyes, making it difficult to see clearly. The thoughts she had kept in abeyance all day came to torment her further in the stillness of the twilight, thrusting their way to the forefront of her mind. With great effort, she pushed them back and forced herself to detach from them. She was too exhausted to think everything through the way she needed to. Sleep, and its promise of sweet escape, was all she desired at that moment.

Chapter 7

She awoke to find herself distanced from where she had originally laid down. The restlessness of her mind was reflected in the apparent unrest of her body. She looked around, and as her eyes adjusted to the light of day, she saw that everything had changed. It was as though a veil had been placed upon her world, obscuring the usual brightness and clarity of her surroundings. Every plant, every beast, and even the sky was now drab and dull to her eyes. A deep sense of sadness and of loss infiltrated her heart. She had developed a love for this place and all of its creatures, but now realized that those feelings had been founded only on what she *thought* she was seeing. She felt that she no longer knew what was true or in what she could trust. She thought she knew Adam, but his words had proven otherwise. In just a brief span of time she had gone from being new to life and feeling like a stranger in an unfamiliar place, to developing a sense of belonging and connectedness, to now perceiving herself as existing separate and alone, estranged from everything she had known and thought to be true in this world.

As she walked, her feelings of desolation only deepened as she regarded that the bleakness she saw had indeed infected the way the entire Garden appeared. What had once been so brilliantly verdant and beautiful was now mundane and bland. All that she had loved seemed to have been a lie. She could hardly bear how terrible it felt. She continued walking, but kept her head down, keeping her eyes focused only on her footsteps as she moved. She was trying not to see the way that her world had changed.

Then, even with her eyes averted, she seemed to glimpse the impression of an area of brightness ahead. She raised her head and quickened her steps, hastening toward it.

Without conscious intention, she had found herself back at the foot of the Tree. She stood before it in astonishment. The way the sun glistened off the edges of each leaf was nearly blinding at first and caused her eyes to squint, yet she found herself unable to remove her gaze from it. She could not understand how she had not immediately seen its exquisite glory the day before. It seemed to stand taller than all of the other trees, and its branches to spread out further, reaching up as if extending itself to the heavens. A flutter of warm excitement began to grow within her belly. It ascended to her chest, and then rose to her throat. The sensation filled her up until it grew so intense that it burst forth out of her mouth in a joyful exclamation. She reached out her hand to touch the Tree. Its knotted bark was cool and calming against her skin. It gave her a sense of solace that dissipated the grayness that had infiltrated her heart. Looking up into its branches and leaves, she was amazed that the sun's light was able to filter through its dense foliage to where she stood at the trunk, but it did. In magnificent streams of light, it did!

She became aware that she was laughing, and found herself suddenly hungry, her stomach no longer filled with tension. She gathered the fruit of another tree, and sat to eat it where she could keep her eyes upon this Tree. Unlike last night, her head now felt remarkably clear, and she was ready to consider Adam's words and what he had meant by them. She replayed all of what he had said slowly in her mind.

It had been devastating for her to listen to him speak of his belief that nature exists as a slavish entity, solely to benefit him. The wound bore even deeper into her heart when he had made it clear that it was not only the plants, animals, rivers, and forests, but that she, too, was created for the purpose of pleasing him. The pain she felt from all of this was only made worse by the fact that she had truly wanted to please Adam, and she had taken joy in his happiness. But these intentions now seemed tainted with the mark of obligation overshadowing their purity. If he believed that she belonged to him, then there could be no trust that her kindness was given with sincerity. It seemed to her that this would somehow limit any satisfaction he could possibly receive from being with her, and she thought that this would be even more disparaging and hurtful to him than to herself. Could he not see that in wanting to rule over her that he was stealing something important from himself? He was destroying the possibility of her genuine love and honor towards him.

She suddenly felt that there was such clarity in the logic of this that a wave of optimism came over her. It seemed so rational, and she was sure that if she just talked to Adam she could make him see it the way she did. She could make him understand. She began to get up so she could rush to find him and resolve this matter between them. Then her glance once again fell upon the Tree, and she realized that there was much more involved than just a misunderstanding in his perspective towards her and towards nature.

Adam's conviction to adhere to the word of God seemed rigid and inflexible. She was disappointed that Adam was not stirred by the same longing to experience the secrets of the Tree.

"How could he not want to understand Good and Evil? And why does he hold on so tightly to a blind faith? Is it a lack of courage on his part that keeps him from taking this step forward, or is he truly satisfied with remaining ignorant to what this Knowledge might be?" she wondered. "And how can it be that he does not see what I see when looking upon the Tree?" As she gazed up at it once more, it appeared even more magnificent. It was as if the sun favored it above all other trees, casting its rays purposely upon it so as to cause each leaf to shimmer as it fluttered in the breeze. Every piece of fruit she saw was a deep, rich purple, so full and ripe, as if it might suddenly burst and spill forth its juices at any moment. A great desire to taste of this Fruit arose within her. But she knew she could not allow this desire to obscure her thinking while she sorted things out. She understood that all things would change after eating it, and once it was done, there was no way to annul the commitment of this act. She turned away from the Tree and found a place to sit where she was distanced from its influence on her senses.

She focused her thoughts on what Adam had told her about God's creating the Tree. The moment she had learned that it was placed here as a test of fidelity, she perceived that a barrier had instantly arisen, cutting her off from everything else. She had been deceived by all that she thought she knew. She tried hard to comprehend the full meaning of the Tree, and to understand why God would beset such a thing before man. She felt that she still knew little of God, only what Adam had said of Him. Adam held his God in such high regard. She wondered if perhaps she herself did not feel this way about God because she had never felt Him speaking directly to her in the way Adam said he had heard God speak to him. She wondered if it was part of God's plan that she be subject to Adam as her teacher, to enforce that she would be dependent on him. Yet it was God's doctrines that she was supposed to follow with a blind faith. It was God's will that she was expected to adhere to and to trust in, even as He blatantly set temptation before her. There was an angry furor that began to grow deep within her the more she considered these things. This was what was at the core of her discord with Adam and with God. It was the root of the conflict within her heart.

"Love", Adam had said. "Our God is a God of love". What she had thought love to be was in conflict with the way Adam had explained the relationship between God and man, and between a man and a woman. Moreover, she was expected to offer her worship and honor to this God? There too, as in her relationship with Adam, were these things not demanded of her and set before her as a test, it would have been easy to give respect and adoration freely. She could not deny all of the wonders that God had created. His masterful Hand had sculpted infinite splendor and beauty, creating even the forms of Adam and of herself. For this, she held a deep gratitude within her heart. But it seemed to her that with the setting forth of the Tree, God Himself had denigrated all of His gifts, including Life. What motive could move Him to do this? What was it that He desired to gain from the existence of the Tree? What were these attributes that He wanted to keep only for the Gods, yet He had placed them before man, as a taunt, within this Tree?

She took a long time in considering these questions, for it seemed that their answers were at the core of her feelings of isolation and deception.

As for the question of His motives in the creation of such a Tree, all that she could conclude was that it really was merely a test to tempt and judge man by. If God did not wish to share the gifts of the Tree, then it should not have been created at all.

"And what of these gifts?" she thought. To eat this sacred Fruit was to acquire the Knowledge of Good and Evil. It seemed to her that if man were able to see things clearly with this Knowledge, it would be ideal. Adam had spoken of God giving them "free will" to choose their actions. The only choice she could see was either to obey His law and remain ignorant of Truth, and to live a sort of half-conscious existence where all beauty and meaning were dulled, as she now saw them, or, they could choose to have their eyes opened and see the true nature of all things. Adam had told her that this latter choice would incur the wrath and vengeance of God and end in death.

Despite her convictions, the longer she contemplated this, the more she began to feel vulnerable and afraid. Even though she could not fully perceive what terrible pain and agony may come with God's punishment, remembering the way Adam had looked and the terrible sound in his voice when speaking of it frightened her. According to Adam, dying meant you no longer feel or experience anything. She had seen carcasses of animals that had died. Their stiff bodies and vacant eyes had disturbed her, and sometimes even made her feel nauseated. She did not want to be like those empty, lifeless bodies. The more Adam's words of death and suffering played over and over in her mind, the more she began to succumb to the panic growing inside her. It took control and consumed her with visions of hideous, lurid things being done to punish her spirit and her flesh. She began to experience sharp, stabbing pain throughout her body. She became deeply anguished at the thought of losing her life, never again taking a breath, never again smelling the fragrance of the flowers carried upon the wind, never again playing in the water, never again seeing her friend, Adam. Her body trembled and shook violently. Her heart pounded fiercely against her ribs, as if it would explode forth from her flesh. Her breath became rapid and unsteady. She began to scream out loud through her tears, over and over "I don't want to die! I don't want to die!"

She then leaped up quickly. She would run to find Adam. She would make amends, and tell him she shall obey God's Law. "Oh my God", she thought, "I don't want to die! I need to go and tell him right now! I so desperately don't want to die! But what direction should I take? How do I find him? I have to find him now!"

Her movements were frenetic and uncoordinated, and she was disoriented with panic. She was so unfocused that she caught her foot upon something that caused her to trip and fall hard to the ground. Fortunately, despite her state, her reflexes had taken over to protect her, and her arms and hands stretched out to brake her fall. She rolled over onto her back, panting to catch her breath. After a time, when she had calmed down, she opened her eyes. She was filled with disbelief at the sight above. Apparently, despite all of her frantic running around, she hadn't gone anywhere. What she had caught her foot on was one of the great roots of the Tree that pushed up through the ground and sprawled around it in serpentine curves. She was lying at the foot of it, looking up into its lush and beautiful branches. All of the terrified thoughts that had been screaming in her head were drowned out by the sound of the wind rustling through its leaves. The scent of the Fruit poured down and washed over her. She inhaled it deeply, and it filled her with a sweet, tranquil happiness. She reached out her hand to once again touch its trunk. She felt as if she were absorbing its strength, and it made her feel strong and rooted in her convictions. All of her fears dissolved away. She saw into her own heart so completely and so clearly in that moment. In being true to herself, there could be no other path. She realized that to choose to live in darkness and ignorance was just another kind of dying- a dying of the spirit. In the rules which God had set forth, either choice extinguished life. If she must die, she would die as herself, not as a creature whose actions were manipulated by fear. Though the consequence that would befall her may be both severe and final, she would choose this way over the illusion of freedom.

"I will seek out Adam to tell him of my choice", she decided, though she knew that his own resolve may be beyond influence, and his desire to adhere to the canons he believes in may be too great to allow him to see the deceptive nature of the counterfeit beauty of Eden. But her heart yearned for him to be able to open himself up to seeing the emptiness of living in this way, so she had to try.

Chapter 8

She found him at the bank of the river, at the same place where he had given her that first drink of water on the day they met. She had known he would be there, because just like her he longed to feel the innocent happiness they had known on that day.

She spoke his name in greeting. The word carried a sound of heavy sadness that she had not intended. They regarded each other in silence for many long moments. She harbored an unfounded hope that the quiet would be broken by a declaration of change on his part. It became evident that this was not to be, and so she broke the silence herself.

"I have come to tell you of the decision I have made. It is no easy thing for me, for I fear that if we cannot agree about the paths we choose, that the dissonance between us will be permanent." She took a deep breath before she continued.

"Adam, I have decided to eat from the Tree. I have searched within myself and have come to know that this is what I must do. There is a force within my heart, at the core of what gives energy to my life, which guides me. Any other way would be acting untrue to myself and would be in conflict with the essence of who I am. Can't you see that when you say 'God has given us free will to choose' it is a lie? There can be no freedom when your options are controlled by fear. If your fidelity to your God brings you this fear and restriction, making you a captive of your faith, then I want no part of it. In your heart, too, you must sense that this is wrong."

His face tightened into a pained expression, and deep furrows appeared across his forehead. His hands clenched onto the hair near his temples as he shook his head side to side. His voice was hoarse and raspy as he implored:

"But why? Why must you push us into this situation? Can you not be satisfied with the bounty He has given us?"

"No!" she cried, "I cannot! And I cannot understand why you would want to remain faithful to such a thing as this! Though all that I have experienced has looked, felt, smelled, and tasted of perfection, it has been nothing but a superficial perception! Beneath the surface, all that is before me now contains a blemish of deceit marring its purity. God has seen fit to feed us and provide for our bodily needs, and though my flesh may grow hale from this bounty, my soul is emaciated from lack of truth to nourish it. Now that I have seen the Tree, I cannot forget or deny its existence. It would be futile to try to contend against my own soul in this matter. There is no victory in a fight against myself. And so, I must eat of the Fruit in order to attain true unity of my body and spirit."

Suddenly, Adam lunged forward, thrusting himself onto his knees before her, grasping her hands in his and crying out:

"Do not do this thing! God will undoubtedly bring suffering and even death for this trespass! You must obey Him, or you will surely perish!"

Tears came into his eyes and spilled down his cheeks. His voice broke as he coughed and choked on his tears. It was torture for her to witness him so. She knew that he feared not only the pain and loneliness he would feel from her death, but she could also see that he grieved over the thought of the pain and agony that she would have to bear if she did this.

A deep sorrow burned within her chest. She knelt down with him, reached out to hold his face in her hands, and drew him in close to her. She spoke very gently to him.

"Adam, I shall forever be grateful that I have known you. You have been my teacher and my friend. Further, it is from the very marrow of your bones that my own flesh was created. My existence is tied inextricably to yours. Yet my soul is my own. There is a spirit that resides within me that cannot be made supplicant to your will, or even to God's. He may smite me and withdraw life's energy from my body, but this choice belongs only to me. I have come to suspect that outside the Garden, in the wilderness you spoke of, it is like this, too. Out there, nature cannot be fully tamed or cultivated to fulfill your bidding. It is wrong, even perverse, for you to be given such absolute power to use, and possibly to harm, the earth at will.

"Also, Adam, I cannot help but recall that you experienced your own discontentment once, as you told me that you took it upon yourself to beseech God to fulfill your desire for a mate. Having done that, you must in some way understand my own longing for something beyond what has been given."

With a biting bitterness in his voice, he answered:

"Yes…yes I did ask the Lord for a mate, and here you are. But if you choose to disobey, it will separate us eternally, and we will be unable to fulfill God's will to perpetuate humankind."

"It is not 'if I choose', Adam, for I am resolved in this matter. And yes, it means we are forever parted," she answered. She did not want to cause him further pain by telling him of the discomfort, no, repulsion, she felt at the thought of engaging in the act of mating that she had witnessed in the animals. To her it had often appeared almost violent or coercive, or at least cold and abrupt. It may be part of the natural order of things among the beasts, she had often thought, but it seemed that it would be wrong, and even degrading, for a man and woman to do this and to bear offspring simply in order to adhere to a commandment. From what Adam had told her it seemed that this was part of God's purpose for them. She sensed that there should be some deeper meaning to it. It did not seem to matter now, however, as she and Adam had determined their separate courses.

Adam appealed to her with one last, desperate plea, "If you do this, and you die, God will send to me another woman to take your place. He will make her more obedient and pious. She will show humility before me and before God. How can you leave me knowing that I will be with another?"

His words brought her to a new, even deeper level of sadness. It was obvious that he had resorted to this measure of hurting her as a final effort to sway her choice. She realized that what he said was probably true, and that there would be another female created in her absence. Perhaps God could make her in such a way that could somehow ensure her piety. Yet this woman would not be her. She saw through Adam's hurtful words, which revealed clearly how much their friendship meant to him. He was in despair, desperately grasping for some means to sway her in order to keep her with him, and keep her safe.

It did not matter how much sympathy she had for him, though, as she could not forget the fact that the Tree existed, and therefore could not falter in her decision. There was no room in her heart for that kind of complacency. Their friendship would then have been rendered meaningless and tinged with resentment. She had decided not to attempt any further effort at influencing or pushing him into choosing as she did. Only Adam could decide what was right for himself.

In response to all that had been both spoken and unspoken between them, she quietly wrapped her arms around him and laid her head against his chest, listening to his strong beating heart. Adam, so exhausted by his pain, did nothing to resist her embrace, and she remained with him in this way for a long while, but ultimately knew that she had to let go. At last, she pulled herself away from the warmth of his body, turned from him, and walked away.

She did not look back.

Chapter 9

As she came within sight of the Tree, her spirit lifted, and she was once again drawn in by its evocative allure. In spite of the excitement she felt at the thought of tasting the Fruit, she maintained an awareness of the gravity of the consequences encompassed within her choice.

She resolved to sit beneath the Tree throughout the night in contemplation of her actions, and to eat nothing more until morning, when she would eat the sacred Fruit. She desired her flesh to be pure and empty of anything other than its influence.

Positioning herself at its base, she crossed her legs and aligned her spine against the ascending trunk. She sat in this way as the sun slipped out of sight, and the moon arose high into the night sky, illuminating both her and the Tree with a mystical glow.

Through the many solitary hours, her mind was engaged in replaying memories and images from her days in the Garden with Adam. Though these days had been few in number, they had been abundantly filled with experience, learning, joy and wonder. She was immensely grateful for all of it.

She knew that it was the Hand of the Creator, God, to whom her gratitude belonged. This made it all the more difficult for her to be at peace and at terms with God. She was in love with Creation, but felt the bitterness of betrayal by its Creator. She could not fully reconcile the conflict this caused within her. She knew the only path for her was the way of Truth and Knowledge. She needed to seek understanding, or all else would be rendered meaningless.

"Why?" she whispered as she looked up toward the starlit heavens. Then her whisper became a shout. "Why would You play such a wicked trick?" She could feel her frustration mounting as she continued to call out. "What kind of God would do such a thing? In doing this You have not ensured my faithfulness! You have instead lighted within me an insatiable desire to eat of this forbidden Fruit and to understand Good and Evil! Perhaps in this act I will come to understand *You*! Where are You and why do You never speak to me? What is this Truth and this Knowledge You wish to keep from us? Speak to me! Speak to me now!"

Her appeals were met only with the nighttime songs of the crickets and frogs while the heavens kept their silence. She eventually calmed down and even drifted off to sleep until she was awakened by the sound of approaching footsteps. The sun was just beginning to rise as she sat up and looked about for Adam. She saw him coming toward her from the direction of the river. She dreaded another emotional episode and did not want things to become even more difficult for either of them. She was about to bid him to leave her, but his words cut her off.

"I did not come to change your decision. I have come to tell you that mine has changed. I have remained awake throughout the night giving great thought to this. The argument I used in order to try to sway you was the very thing that moved my own heart to shift. When I contemplated another woman to replace you, I experienced a horrible and acrid emptiness. My heart would be as a stone to any other but you. It is the image of you that shall always be impressed upon me, as a seal upon my heart. Just as you say you cannot carry on an existence true to yourself unless you follow this path of Knowing, I cannot live fully as myself if I forsake you. I will be your friend and act as one with you in this choice. Your fate shall also be my own."

She was so overcome that she dared not break the moment with words. She simply reached up and pulled a piece of the Fruit from the lowest branch. It was perfectly ripe and its flesh was full and heavy. She touched it to her lips, and breathed in deeply. Its essence caused a smile upon her lips. Her mouth pierced through its purple skin, and its sweet juices ran down her chin. She closed her eyes so she could shut out everything except the taste and feel of it on her tongue. She savored this experience for many moments, lingering within the sensation it gave her. At last, she could draw the moment out no further, as the desire for this Fruit to be fully taken in and become a part of her could no longer be denied. When she swallowed, the feeling of being completely fulfilled and nourished was beyond anything she could have anticipated.

Her greatest desire now was to share this with Adam. She realized that if he hadn't come to her, she would have run to him. This taste of ecstasy was a gift meant to be shared and given freely. She understood that this was part of the Knowledge of what is Good.

Adam took a bite of the Fruit offered from her hands. This rekindled the memory of drinking the water he had offered her from his own hands at the bank of the river on her first day of life. It gave her the impression of having come full circle with Adam, and she could sense that together they had embarked upon a new season of their life together.

They continued eating more of the Fruit, until their bellies were full and they could eat no more. Then Adam looked upon her and spoke.

"I feel there is a part of my being that either did not exist before this day, or had lain dormant, as if dead. A sense of divinity has been awakened within me. Though my flesh was created by God, it is you, woman, who has offered me the gift of true life. This form of mine was vacant, but through the inspiration of your fearless act, my eyes have been opened. Where I once was empty and restricted, there now exists a soul.

"It has been a shame upon me that I have been unable to ascribe a name to you that is befitting of who you are. Now that the Fruit has allowed me to see the true nature of all things, I am able to clearly see the truth of your essence. You shall be called 'Eve'."

As he spoke this beautiful new word, her name, she felt her heart ignite with a fierce burning from the overwhelming loveliness of it. She barely managed to whisper through the tears that it brought, "What does it mean?"

"It means 'Mother of the Living'," he answered. "This is who you are, as you have not only ignited my life, but you shall be the mother of all generations to come, and your children shall be born of love.

"But this is not all that I see when I look upon you. There are many qualities about you which I have become awakened to. I now see how beautiful you are, and to look upon you stirs within me a desire I have never before known."

Eve's perception of Adam had also undergone a shift now that they had shared the Fruit. He had demonstrated an inner strength by his actions. He did not falter because of fear of God; rather, he acted with virtue and faithfulness to his heart, and to her. Her trust in him had become absolute, allowing her to see how these qualities seemed to have become manifest in his body. His form, which had always appeared so firm, yet rigid in its strength, emanated a more fluid and even greater vitality. It was a strength that she wanted to experience and feel.

Adam, too, wanted to experience Eve. He reached his hand to the back of her neck, and pulled her to him. His mouth connected with hers, and he parted her lips with his tongue. He drew her in, ever deeper with his kiss as their hands explored each other's bodies. They had touched before, but never in this way. Every cell of her body was charged with an ecstatic current, and all she could think was that she wanted more…more of this feeling…more kisses from his mouth…more of his hands moving across her soft skin…more of his earthy scent… *More…*

He pulled her down to the ground with him, and as they lie beneath the shade of the Tree, she savored the sensual pleasure of his weight upon her. The influence of his body swept over her, and she met his firmness and strength with supplication. Her flesh yielded completely to his.

Instinctively she understood what was about to happen, and she realized that she had been entirely wrong before in not wanting to experience this with Adam. This was a wholly unique expression from what she had seen the animals engage in. Now that her eyes had been opened, she desired this more than she ever would have expected.

With every inhalation, her breasts rose up and pressed deeply against Adam's chest. His face touched hers, and she could feel his warm sweet breath against her ear, causing her own breath to change in response, becoming synchronized with his rhythm.

He pushed up onto his elbows, raising his head above hers to look upon her. Held in each other's gaze, they revealed themselves completely to each other; their naked souls mirroring their naked bodies. Eve opened herself up to him, and flesh became immersed into flesh.

Breathing as with one breath, moving as with one body, together they entered into love's holy space. Their energy escalated and cycled in vibrant rhythms between their bodies, until it surged and erupted into the blissful culmination of release.

With the midday sun suffusing its warmth into their naked skin, fulfilled happiness carried them into sleep. For Eve, it was the most lovely sleep that she had ever known, a sleep that was without dreams of far away origins or past existence. She was firmly rooted in the experience of what existed for her then and there.

She awoke a short time later with a gentle start at seeing Adam looking upon her intently.

"I love you Eve.

His words were not mere words. They were somehow tangible entities which seemed to absorb into her body and become fused with her heart, causing it to ache in its fullness. He continued speaking to her in a soft, low tone

"I have used the word 'love' before, but as I speak it now, it seems a new discovery to me. Just as the meaning in all things has become new to me because of you.

"Within the communion of our flesh, love has become manifest. No longer an emotion, but a sanctified offering. Even as I named you 'Eve, Mother of the Living', I was not yet aware of how profoundly you have unlocked my soul to what it is to be truly alive. In making love with you, I have been born. To enter into your body is to enter into life itself.

"I love you as my very breath. I inhale the sweetness of your scent and fill my lungs to take in more of the air that has dwelled in the atmosphere of you. My eyes are blessed at the sight of you, wanting nothing more than to behold the dark and lovely hue of your skin, the fullness of your lips, and the grace of your every motion, arousing my desire. My eyes are further blessed to see your eyes meeting my gaze with a radiance that reflects your same desire for me. Nothing could mean more to me than this.

"You are as a field of wildflowers which have at this moment come into full bloom. You open yourself to me as petals open to the sun. I taste the nectar of your lips and become intoxicated by the fragrance within your garden. There are secrets I could not have imagined that lie below your navel and within the curve of your hips. Wonderful, sweet secrets."

His words aroused her longing for the sensual experience of his body. What he said was true. She was a field of flowers, which he had caused to flourish. As his mouth again laid delicate kisses upon her neck and her breasts, he entered ever more deeply into her, and all of the petals were induced to once again unfurl into fullness.

The more fully she surrendered, the more complete was their fusion. Their kinetic energy became amplified with each fluent motion, and she could feel the surge of Adam's vital, potent life force as it became integrated with her own. This energy circulated throughout her core and ascended, rising to her chest, her heart, her head, and then radiated outward. With her kiss, the sensual flow circulated back to Adam, completing the cycle.

Eve grew hot and flushed as her excitement heightened. The sounds of their passion and the sighs of love's divine song were carried on the wind to mingle among the branches of the trees. Ecstasy's rapturous spark caused its current to pulse throughout their bodies, too strong and too expansive to be contained. Its heat exuded out from their flesh, causing the air around them to become consecrated by the mist that arose from their skin. A final cry of passion escaped through Eve's parted lips.

*   *   *

As she lay with her head upon Adam's chest, her heart, already replete with love and ecstasy, felt nearly unable to bear the immense swell of emotion as she noticed that Eden once again appeared bright and verdant. All around her were the joyful sounds of the animals and birds, and the scent of the lush flowering underbrush filled the air.

She was lulled to sleep for the second time that day by the sound of Adam's beating heart and the soporific warmth of his skin. She felt wrapped in contented, blissful perfection.

Chapter 10

Peace and joy were violently ripped away by a thunderous roar, emanating from both above and below. They were torn from slumber to find that the once blue sky had turned an oppressive grey, casting the world beneath a dark and loathsome shadow. The air was heavy, damp, and stagnant, with a repulsively sour, fetid stench that clung to their skin, leaving its foul residue. The earth quaked fiercely, as if about to rupture and split open to swallow them up. All of this they took for the wrath of an angry God.

Eve and Adam stood together, struggling to maintain their balance amidst the chaos that surrounded them. Adam wrapped his arms around Eve, holding her tightly against his body to help keep her steady.

"God is coming," he said. "I fear only for you. I do not fear my own death, for I will gladly pay the price of this flesh's mortality for the gift I have been given of knowing what is Good, and experiencing your love with my eyes opened by the trespass of gaining this holy Knowledge.

Eve answered, "I, too, would give my very life as exchange for eating the Fruit. We have become gnostic of ourselves and of one another, able now to see the unique and beautiful Truth in our nakedness. I hold my nakedness sacred, for only you to behold. I do not want God to look upon us in judgment, so let us clothe ourselves, and keep our bodies exclusive to one another."

Adam agreed with this, and despite the constant quavering tremors of the ground they managed to gather large fig leaves, along with long blades of grass, pliant enough to be woven into simple coverings for their loins. Eve used her hair as a veil upon her breasts.

Just as abruptly as it had begun, the onslaught of thunder and quaking ceased, and the world became shrouded in a heavy silence. All was unnaturally still, as if no living thing dared to defy the hush. The animals had disappeared from sight, and the Garden felt empty and devoid of life. There was a strange, surreal quality to everything, and even the passing of time felt as if it had been altered, succumbing to the will of God. Eve clutched at her abdomen as it roiled and churned with a sick dread.

The silence grew ever more unbearable until at last it was shattered as a violent wind, which could only have been the Breath of God, swept across the sky, dispelling the heavy clouds. Yet, the sight of the sky remained obscured from them. All they could perceive was a brilliant supernal light that glowed like white fire pouring down from the heavens. It bathed them and all of Creation in its frightening glory.

The wind bellowed and sang with the Voice of God. To Eve it was both terrifying and beautiful, bringing her down onto her knees as it pulsed through her in pounding waves. Even as she struggled to steel herself against the overwhelming tempest of sound and vibration, the manifest fury of God's curses, she found herself enveloped within a sense of blessed sanctification. Eve felt she could finally hear God speaking to her.

This magnificent revelation came with a nearly unbearable mix of pleasure and agony. She felt simultaneously as though her soul were being lifted up to Heaven, while at the same time her heart was being savagely gripped and squeezed by some great and powerful hand until it would ultimately be strangled and destroyed.

When finally the perdition came to an end, with the storm passing and the world once again falling silent, Eve and Adam both collapsed to the ground. It felt as though God's malice had dissolved their muscles and bones through their flesh. They were rendered feeble and limp, and lay as if dead...

But they were not dead. In God's reckoning, they could foresee that there would be great pain and sorrow to be endured throughout the remainder of their days. Yet, they would have days. They knew not why, but God had not taken their lives from them that day. God had made them mortal, and death was imminent, but not there, not then. Even as she lay in her battered and bewildered state, Eve was grateful.

*   *   *

Both Adam and Eve felt that misery and ruin were all that could be left for them in Eden. They felt cursed to leave behind the life they had known... the bounty and beauty of the Garden, the closeness they felt with the animals with whom they shared Eden, the days filled with a carefree sense of safety and certainty, the ease of an existence where all was provided... all of these things were now a part of their past. When they had recovered their strength, they gathered what food they could carry and made their departure from Eden.

Chapter 11

Their banishment from Eden was necessary, for they made the choice to act upon what they believed to be a sin against God, and it is what a man believes that gives meaning to his actions. Their punishments were the manifest fulfillment of their beliefs and expectations. '*Ask, and thou shall receive.*' Man had asked for dogma and restriction, wanting to believe in cannons, rewards, and punishments, and so, it had to be.

God could foresee the hardships the people would bear in living forever divided from Eden. They would be severed from the harmony between man and beast, man and the land, and even peace between men, for these things would not always come easily outside of Eden. Man would need to strive for this harmony, requiring the volition of his spirit to inspire the actions of his flesh in order to attain them.

Unto Adam would befall the hardship and trials of labor. By the sweat of his brow, he shall struggle against thistle and thorn to cultivate the land for his nourishment. And despite long years of laboring in the soil to provide sustenance for himself and his family, still he shall ultimately perish. His flesh shall return to the same dust and clay from which it was formed.

Both Adam and his wife shall suffer enmity between man and beast. Man shall continue to strive for dominion over all things wild, but there will be distrust of man by the animals, causing conflict and competition for man's place in Nature. However, it would remain the immutable responsibility of all men to care for and tend to the animals, and also to be mindful of the earth, the sky, and the water. If Adam or his descendants fail in their role as guardians and caretakers, then it shall come to be that Nature will begin to turn her back on man. If man does not hearken to these signs, and should continue to lack respect for what he has been blessed with, becoming ever more careless in his responsibilities, failing as keeper of the earth in successive generations, he shall be made to suffer greatly as Nature will reflect back to him the consequences of his arrogant ways. There will be illness and starvation, brought about by man's own heedlessness. The air shall become thick and heavy, choking him. The water shall become impure, and be as poison to his body. The wonders and beauty of life contained in the forms of animals and plants will begin to disappear from his world, and leave man with nothing but a vast wasteland which he himself created.

But it was the suffering which would afflict the woman which imbued God's heart with the deepest level of grief. It shall be with great pain and sorrow, both of the body and of the spirit, that she brings forth life from her womb.

This curse upon the woman mirrored the agonies of God's own heart, for woman seemed condemned to endure what God endures in His longing for intimacy with the human life created from His own essence. Woman would be allowed to experience the profound beauty and ecstasy of creating life within her womb, only to have the potential for this divinity marred by the curse of agony and longing. The desire within a woman's heart to give love and to nurture others would be the very instruments of despair and sadness in her life if those she chooses to love should turn away from her.

Yet, God also knew that man need not be lost to bleakness and despair. For in the limitlessness of the Universe, there always lies a choice, and there always exists unbounded opportunity.

Intrinsically woven within each curse exists the potential for blessings. Blessings designed in such a way that they could be attained through sapient use of the Knowledge of Good that the man and woman had gained. By man's own virtuous actions, he could transpose that which was his burden into that which would be his redemption. Man could obtain a renewed state of purity within his soul, and be brought once again to live within a state of grace.

God recognized that it was Good for the people to have eaten the Fruit, for in doing so, man had become free. Because man had chosen to see things with opened eyes, rather than follow with blind faith, he would be free to determine his own fate. He could be bound by deprivation and misery, or he could use the Knowledge gained from choosing to eat from the Tree to create love and give meaning to his days.

God, too, was free. Free from the shackles of blame that men may be tempted to place upon Him for both their blessings and their woes. It would remain to be seen, through the course of each man's life, his capacity to see this truth and to embrace or deny the freedom which is his.

And so, the story continues…

Part II

Chapter 12

The heat caused her to awaken. It was far too oppressive, even in the early hours of morning, to allow for any further sleep.

Several days had passed since their exodus from the Garden. When they had departed Eden they kept their eyes forward, to the East, without looking back. Since then, they had traversed across a vast desert that they hadn't even known existed. A land where the sun blazed without mercy, burning their skin, and the wind blew the coarse sand into their throats and their eyes. Their lips had become so dry as to crack and split open, heal, and split again many times over. Eve refused to believe that outside of the Garden this was all that existed. She could not betray the hope in her heart that in time the landscape would change.

Food and water had been meager, but on rare occasions they had come upon sparse groupings of plants, and by digging to the ends of their roots, they had uncovered small springs of water. Barely enough to sustain them, and not nearly enough to quell their deep thirst. Yet somehow, in perhaps a cruel way, it was always just enough to nurture their hope and keep them going.

The now familiar birds of prey had already begun circling overhead as they did each day, serving not as a sign of life above, but instead signaling the anticipation of death. Their cries for carnage rang hollow through the arid desert sky. They could not be begrudged this, however, for the death of another was a necessity for their own survival. Adam and Eve tried to disregard the presence of the scavenger birds as they prepared for another day of walking. This meant trying to reposition the coverings on their bodies, which were their only vestiges of the life they had known in Eden. Each day, these woven leaves became drier, and it would only be a matter of time before they would crumble off of their bodies and fall as dust to the ground.

As they crossed the desert land, they remained mostly silent, reserving their energy for the continual effort of walking. When they had first begun their journey, they had sometimes found caves set within the limestone hill formations that surrounded them. They would rest in these dark caves during the day and move in the cooler nighttime. But it had been days since they had come upon any more caves, or any other source of shade, so there was no choice but to continue by day, for it would have been impossible to sleep beneath the scorching sun, which allowed for no comfort or rest. And so it was that they endured the perilous desert throughout each day, and each day had become the same. Step after step, both the passing of time and the tedium of the desert were drawn out endlessly.

In the beginning, Eve's thoughts had dwelled on Eden, and a part of her mourned inside at the loss, even though she believed that she herself had caused their exile. But she knew that she would not have changed her actions, even now. And as the days continued to wear on, Eden had almost ceased to have existed for her, as if it had only been a part of some strange and elusive dream. Its image had become warped and faded, just as the sun and heat seemed to have warped and faded all the workings of her mind. Her capacity for rational thought had diminished in response to hunger, thirst, fatigue, and sadness. Brief moments of lucidity only taunted her by making her aware that throughout most of her hours she was lost in confusion and detachment. Perhaps the confusion was a gift, she sometimes thought, as it took the place of her only reality, which was the sand and the sun. The endless, cruel, unforgiving sand, and the wicked, relentless sun.

Still, they kept going, as it was all they could do. Eventually, their shadows grew long with the passing of another day where each step and each moment was cursed. Eve was about to say to Adam that she could go no further, when he abruptly stopped. He looked as if he were studying something in the distance and held up his hand as a sign for her to be still. At first she only perceived the monotonous hum of the desert wind, but then, there was perhaps something else. As the wind struck at her face, she began to sense a slight difference. There was something in the way the air felt, and even smelled, that had been nearly forgotten by her, but was distinctively familiar. Recognition and realization slowly came upon her. The air carried the subtle scent of something fresh, something alive and green. Instead of relief at what this could signify, she was at first wary and suspicious. Many times one of them had believed they were witnessing the sight of water, or trees, or some other sign of life, only to discover that their own senses had betrayed them. The desert seemed to mock them in its influence over their perceptions. On those occasions, though, only one of them was deceived, while the other was still able to see the truth. Now, she thought, either they both were suffering under the same delusion or, finally, they might truly be saved.

As she looked into Adam's eyes, she saw the truth and reality of the moment reflected back at her through his expression. As they shared this glimmer of hope, she felt that she was seeing Adam anew. It was as though they had been parted for a long time, each of them wandering the desert in a solitary existence, lost to each other within the shadows of their own thoughts. But now, this faint detection of promise carried upon the wind was enough to spark the return of life into their souls, reconnecting them to themselves and to each other. Adam smiled at her through burned and blistered lips as he reached out and took her hand. They both looked to the direction of the wind, straining their eyes to try to see something other than sand and sky.

"There is something, I think, beyond that far dune," he said, but his words were then cut off as he began coughing furiously. He had not spoken for days, and it was a strain for him to overcome the dryness of his throat to say anything more.

Wordlessly, they walked on, and for a time Eve seemed able to disregard all of her pain and fatigue. But soon it became apparent that the dune was much further away than it had first appeared. Though she and Adam were now moving faster than they had their entire journey, they were still unable to get to the dune quickly enough to satisfy her desperate longing. And when at last they finally did reach it, they found it to be a vast, seemingly unending wall of sand. The sun had already begun its descent in the late afternoon sky as they embarked on their climb up the great hill. Eve's feet sunk in with each step, and it was difficult work for her muscles to overcome how the sand gave way beneath her, pulling her slightly downward and back with each step she tried to take forward. Outwardly she struggled, but inside she could feel a sense of defiant perseverance silently building, for she knew that they were close to the end of this desert hell, and there was nothing short of death that could stop her from reaching the source of that fresh new wind.

As they ascended the highest plateau of the great mountain of sand, they could see an outlined area of darkness in the far distance ahead of them which they knew signified trees. But were it not for the last hint of twilight, it would not have been visible at all. At that height, with nothing to block the direct path of the breeze, Eve took in several deep breaths, as if she were drinking in the wind and swallowing it down. The air soothed her dry and dusty lungs and cooled her burned skin. It also caused her body to relax, however, and the extent of her exhaustion suddenly overwhelmed her. She looked to Adam, and he let out a deep sigh. They both seemed to acknowledge that there was still a significant distance to cross before they would be among those trees.

Adam said, "Though it pains me to stop when we have come so far, it is too dark to continue on. Perhaps it is best if we descend the dune and complete the remainder of our journey in the light of the morning. We know not what we may find there, and we both have grown weary despite our desire to go on."

It disappointed her, but she agreed with Adam, and they made their way down the other side of the sand hill. Though it was faster than their climb up, the descent was far more treacherous. They stumbled and slid much of the way, their skin becoming even more scathed and raw and imbedded with sand. Once they were at the bottom, they lay upon the ground which had already begun to grow cooler in the evening air. They huddled close to share the warmth of each other's bodies against the chill of the desert night. And though it was the same abrasive sand that had ground against her skin night after night, Eve did not care. Tomorrow, she would be going somewhere different. A place which held for them the promise of a new beginning.

*　　　　　*　　　　　*

As the sun began to rise, Eve was already up, eager and ready to end their journey, believing in her heart that whatever lay ahead would have to be better than where they had been.

For a while, all they could see ahead of them was that same vague appearance of a dark area, contrasted with the rest of the landscape, which held only the endless nothingness of the desert. As they walked on, and the hours of the day passed, the darkness ahead lightened to green, and eventually they could discern the contrasting shapes and shades among the trees. Beneath their feet the color and texture of the earth was changing, becoming richer and more dense as soft dirt came to gradually replace the rough grains of sand. With increasing frequency, there were patches of grass shooting up from the ground, and as they continued, they began to pass by small bushes. These were scattered and sparse at first, but soon there came to be thick brush growing all around them. Eve caught a glimpse of a brightly patterned snake darting beneath one of the plants, fleeing to seek safety from her footsteps. She was momentarily taken back by this, as no living thing in Eden had ever turned or fled from their approach. This thought was transient, however, and she found herself filled with happiness as they walked through the thick foliage, with its layered textures and shades of green that did not appear so different from what she had known in the Garden. As they continued to move through the forest, there was no doubt that they were coming nearer to water. The air had grown dewy and was scented with rich moss and fern. The joyful songs of birds resounded from all directions as Adam and Eve explored this new place, absorbing its beauty and feeling the energy of the life it contained after knowing only the arid desolation of the desert for so long.

They had been following the sound of moving water as they wended their way through the trees. Though she knew they were getting close to its source, nothing could have prepared Eve for the rush of emotion that overtook her as they emerged from within the shade of the forest and her eyes beheld the great river before her. Her legs staggered, causing her to grasp onto Adam to steady herself and keep from falling forward, as she was so physically and emotionally overwhelmed by the sudden realization that she had truly survived the hell of their expulsion from Eden. God, it seemed, had not damned them forever. She hadn't let herself acknowledge the depth of her despair and fear while in the desert, but it all swelled up within her as she looked to this river that seemed the culmination of their journey. This was what the days of suffering had at last led them to.

The urgency to drink overcame both of them. They ran to the water and knelt at its bank. Eve drank in as fast as she was able, handful after handful, until her belly began to ache and swell. Though they did not know it, this river stemmed from one of the four born out of the Garden, though here it flowed much colder than the waters within Eden. The chill could not stop Eve from immersing herself, and Adam followed her. The initial sting of the cool water upon their burned skin soon gave way to feelings of relief and renewal. They let the water wash away the dust, the grit, and the despair that the desert had left on them. The river carried it all away, leaving them clean. The last remnants of their coverings were also removed by the flowing water, swept away along the current.

Though it was pleasurable to be naked in the water, Eve had come to realize during the time when her flesh was partially covered the true sacredness she felt in her nakedness, as well as in Adam's, and she decided to continue to cover portions of her flesh at times when she was not bathing, swimming, or sharing intimacy with him. She spoke this intention to him, and added:

"It is not because of God's eyes that I choose to do this. I have come to realize that no weaving of vine or reed could keep us hidden from God, who intimately knows every inch of our forms. I choose to do this because of my own desire to keep with exception that which is unique and mysterious in each of us."

Adam sighed and smiled at her, saying "Eve, if it is because of fear that my eyes will tire of you, or become accustomed to your beauty that you do this, know that this could never be. You grow more desirable with each glance I cast upon you. Not even the desert's harshness could taint or intrude upon your exquisite perfection.

"However," he continued, "I do see practical reasons to continue to clothe ourselves. Though we are no longer in the extreme elements of the desert, we are in an unknown place that is surely not as benign as Eden. It may be wise to protect our skin in this measure. Though dried and sparse, I was glad for the coverings that we had left to us while we were exposed to the desert sun and wind. We cannot take for granted that God will protect us from harm, and should do what we can to keep ourselves safe in this new land."

Eve felt a shiver pass through her at hearing his words. She had let herself become momentarily disillusioned by the relief and joy of finding this place, allowing herself to forget that it would be different from the life they had known in Eden.

Chapter 13

After they had finished bathing, they climbed out of the river to lie upon the soft earth and warm themselves in the sun. It was not long before their stomachs began rumbling from hunger. They rose up to explore the trees and gather food. Most of the fruits that they found were familiar to them, similar to the fruits of Eden, but there were also many types of small berries and herbs which Eve had never seen before. She asked Adam what they were, and he told her that many of these were unknown to him as well. He was very troubled by this, as he had known of all things that lived and grew in Eden.

"Here is further proof that this wilderness will bring to us many new difficulties. It remains man's task to know and to name the plants and beasts, though now it can only be done by observation of each to discover its essence and learn of its qualities. It seems clear that the world outside of the Garden is wrought with danger and uncertainty, and that the nature of things here is of change and survival, unlike the constancy of Eden. Now we both must take care to learn about each new thing so we can determine what is safe for us."

Adam's words troubled Eve, and though she said nothing aloud, she could not keep from wondering, "Is there to be conflict and strife in every aspect of my existence?" It seemed so, for each time she had felt her spirit ascend and her heart fill with joy, there had been some way in which those feelings were seized from her possession. As she saw it, her happiness had been taken by God time and time again.

It had begun at the moment she became a woman and was set upon this earth. She felt that before becoming flesh and blood, her energy had been part of a different existence, connected with all things as part of the boundlessness of infinity. It seemed to her that the visions she often experienced in her dreams were deeply rooted memories of that time. It was as if she were witnessing her own creation in those dreams, and it made her feel as though she had lost something when she had become bound by the limitations of the flesh. The sadness of that loss was lessened by the many wonders she had found in Eden and the connection she felt with all that lived in the Garden, though mostly it was her friendship with Adam that had made her feel happiness and security in this existence.

Then, upon learning of the Tree she felt that her happiness had been hollow; merely a response to what she *thought* was true. This false veil that had been cast upon Eden by God had nearly severed her friendship with Adam and had caused her to feel alone and once more as a stranger in this world. But eating the Fruit had lifted this veil and allowed her eyes to open and her heart to be elevated to a state of ecstasy. Her spirit had been reopened to the experience of what it is to dwell within the greatness of the universe when her flesh and spirit merged with Adam's in the act of love. Through this union with him, she had discovered a path toward reintegrating her spirit with the origin of all things, and she felt once again as if her soul knew no boundaries.

But God had revoked that joy, too, with His curses. Her exultation had been countered by exile. Her heart had descended into a despair that mirrored the harsh emptiness of the desert. Foolish as it seemed, she had allowed herself once more to experience hope and relief at coming upon this land with its flowing river surrounded by lush forest. With Adam's warning she felt once again that her spirit was denied reprieve from the trials of life. Every time she had tasted joy there seemed to be a bitterness that followed.

Eve continue to linger within her silent thoughts throughout the day, barely aware of anything else around her as she sat on the grassy bank of the river, lulled by the sound of its constant movement. This same river that had caused her to feel so much excitement when they first saw it, now seemed to be just another symbol of what appeared to her to be a futile existence. She wondered if there was to be an act of penance as restitution for every occasion of peace or happiness she was given. She did not want to fully resign herself to believing this was so.

She was only vaguely aware of Adam's presence beside her, as they both had remained quiet as the day had passed them by. There seemed no use to giving voice to her despair. She did not know if Adam felt all of these things as she did, but perhaps he dwelled on similar thoughts, and that was the reason that he, too, kept his silence.

The sun had all but disappeared without her realizing that the day was nearing its end. She stirred from her sedentary state and looked over to Adam. He was stretched out upon the grass, and looked to be on the edge of sleep. Perhaps she had been lightly drifting in and out of sleep as well, for when she arose she was groggy and had difficulty focusing. Adam sensed her movement and his eyes blinked open. He stood up next to her and said, "It has grown cold here by the water. Let us go find a place to sleep within the forest where it should be warmer."

As they made their way back through the trees they could hear the nocturnal calls of the animals. When they had passed through the forest earlier that day to get to the river, they had been aware of the sounds of the animals moving around them, and had caught occasional fleeting glimpses of the beasts observing them through the trees and bushes. They had been focused then only on reaching the water, and had not given much consideration to the animals. Now however, there was a pounding within Eve's chest, and her stomach tightened with a kind of fear she had not known before at the sounds of these howls and cries. The palms of her hands and her forehead were damp, and she gripped tightly onto Adam's arm.

Though he showed no outward signs of fear, Adam too felt wary and anxious.

"Perhaps it is best if we walk back to the edge of the forest and do not sleep within its depths after all. Let us pull down large leaves and branches so that we can lean them against the trunk of a tree to create a shelter to sleep within."

Their labor did not come easy for them, but in time they had constructed a makeshift shelter that seemed adequate to keep them concealed for the night.

Sleep only came to Eve in brief intervals, which were frequently severed by the sudden calls that pierced through the night. Some came as echoes from a distance, but others sounded unnervingly near. Her breath and heartbeat quickened, causing her to lie awake for long periods in heightened vigilance. Though they spoke no words and made no movements out of caution of betraying themselves to any of the predators, Eve knew that Adam lay awake just as she did at those times, and she suspected that he did not allow himself even the brief moments of rest she had been somehow able to fall into. He was protective and watchful over her. That was his nature.

The animals eventually quieted, and Eve's fatigue had at last overtaken her in the hours before the rising of the sun. She found herself waking from a sleep filled with frightening dreams and visions such as she had never before experienced. The morning's soft light filtered in through the leaves as she looked upon Adam. It was clear by the redness and swelling of his eyes that he indeed had not allowed himself any rest. She suggested that they go together to gather their morning's food, and after they had eaten she insisted that Adam sleep some more. He agreed, but told her that while he slept he wished for her to remain close and not venture alone until they had come to better know this land and all that dwelled within it. Though she felt something reminiscent of her first days in Eden, when she had been so eager to explore and discover her surroundings, she knew that he was right and it would be best to learn the ways of this wilderness with caution.

While Adam slept, Eve decided to weave new coverings for their bodies. When in Eden, they had clothed themselves using the leaves of the Tree. But those garments had not served well as protection from the sun and the wind. In considering what could now be used, she decided that the long, softer grasses that grew near the water could easily be woven together.

Eve was eager to begin, so she started out toward the river to gather what she needed. She knew that Adam would be cross with her for wandering even that short distance, so she moved very quickly and cautiously. She returned with a large bundle of grasses and began her work. As she sat and twined the fibrous plants together, she watched the brilliantly colored birds and the small scurrying animals as they searched for food on the ground and among the bushes. They sometimes scuttled about after each other, giving chase in a way that appeared to be simply for play rather than for territory or dominance. Eve had often enjoyed watching these games of the animals in Eden, and was delighted to find this similarity here. The animals at first seemed to maintain a cautious distance from her, but as time passed, and as long as she did not move too suddenly, they gradually began to come nearer to where she was. She smiled as she felt the weight of darkness that had plagued her throughout the previous day and night begin to dissolve.

As she continued to watch the small creatures, she noticed that there were certain bushes whose berries the animals would go to and investigate, but they would never eat them; instead they would move on to a different bush where they would eat freely. She guessed that there must be a scent or some other quality that turned them away, and that whatever it was could be something that signified harm to them, and would be dangerous for her and Adam as well.

She told Adam about this later as he arose and stretched out his limbs, shaking off the remnants of sleep.

"It is good that you have seen this," he said. "We must observe all things new to us in this way. We have eaten fruits here that are familiar to us, and this we may continue to do. However, those berries you saw the birds turn from did not grow in Eden. Furthermore, we both have sensed that something is very different here than what we have known in regard to the animals. One of our curses to bear is the distrust between man and beast, and it is up to man to re-establish his place among the animals, as well as within all of Creation. As you have witnessed, the birds and smaller creatures flee at our approach, but come nearer when we remain quiet and still, thus showing them that we are not to be feared. Though this of itself saddens me, I sense that there may be a more severe consequence of our division from the animals. It is what caused our reaction to the sounds of the animals that prowl and hunt by night. We have witnessed that the balance of life includes both predator and prey among the species for survival, but we were exempt from this when in Eden, where we experienced a divine harmony with all creatures. I have come to feel a troubling instinct of fear arise within me that has never before existed.

"And though this fear is strong, it is but nothing when compared to the grief I feel at this loss. It does not seem possible that there is no hope of regaining the peace we have known in living with the animals. Now that the natural harmony between us has been weakened, I deeply regret my past lack of understanding and respect for man's relationship with the beasts.

"Let not our desire to regain this harmony make us unwary, however. Instead, let us go observe the way of things. Through learning to understand the ways of this wilderness we may come to discover how to regain some of that which has been lost to us."

They began to journey through the forrest, and after having passed through the thick trees, the atmosphere shifted from the sultry warmth of the forest to the dryer, more intense heat caused by the direct sunlight shining brightly upon the open glade to which they had come. Looking across the distance of the tall grasses, Eve saw that the river continued to wind its way through this part of the land, and there was a herd of antelope grazing near it. Adam took her hand and led her across the glade until they came upon a tree that stood somewhat apart from the others. He had chosen it for this reason and for its branches, which appeared sturdy and were low enough for them to easily climb. He helped Eve ascend the tree and then followed her up. There they had an unobstructed view of the herd across the clearing, as well as a clear vantage of the snaking path of the river.

From their high perch, they enjoyed the peacefulness of watching the gentle antelope graze, but it was not long before the scene of tranquility changed. Though they knew it was part of the natural order of life, they both felt a certain sense of dread when they saw the great cat approach slowly from the west. With calculated stealth, she moved in to stalk her prey. The herd remained unaware, and Eve felt a pang of guilt that she could foresee what they could not. The beast's movements were graceful, fluid and precise as she prowled quietly through the grasses, carefully keeping herself hidden from her prey.

Suddenly, she bound forth into the herd, scattering them in all directions, and it did not take her long to overcome one of the antelope. She easily took it down, felling it onto its side. Her jaws latched on, penetrating deep into its flesh. Blood spilled forth as the beast tore tendon and muscle from bone. The animal flailed and bucked, but was unable to escape its fate. There had been two more great cats lying in wait, taking their opportunity when the herd had scattered. They, too, had made successful kills and were sating their hunger for flesh, boring their teeth into the flanks of the animals as they ripped out chunks of meat. Their bloodied muzzles glistened with a bright crimson luster in the sunlight.

Eve's heart was beating wildly, though not solely from fear. It was something of a different quality; a strange and unbidden combination of emotions in response to the brutal scene, and she was disturbed by it. She turned to look at Adam and saw upon his face the magnified reflection of her feelings in his own expression. His pupils were dilated, intent and avid. His jaw was set hard, and his mouth appeared lustful and hungry as his teeth bit down into his lower lip. His chest heaved with strong quickening breaths. He was mesmerized and bound by the spell of witnessing such power and ferocity. It unsettled Eve to know that moments ago she had looked as he did, entranced and excited by the carnage.

She turned her eyes back upon the scene and found that more of the clan had come to share in the bounty of the hunt. They appeared to be vying for the choicest position from which to feed. One in particular was edged out by the others. His stature was somewhat smaller than the rest, though he did not appear to be one of their young. His status was obviously lower because of his size. He stood down from the others and surveyed the area. As Adam and Eve were not very high up in the tree, where the dense leaves could have hidden them better, it was not difficult for them to be spotted. The beast began to lope toward them, looking at first more curious than vicious. Eve and Adam were of one mind, however, as they both moved to climb higher up into the tree simultaneously. They had wished to learn the extent of the trust and harmony they could now have with the beasts through observation, not by the blood of trial and error.

The cat approached the base of the tree, pacing back and forth in front of it several times before he suddenly stopped and leapt upward, stretching his front legs and lengthening his torso so that he reached to the height of where their own legs had been just moments before. He roared and snarled at them, baring his teeth and leaving no uncertainty in the pit of Eve's stomach of his intent. He made several more attempts to vault himself upward toward them, and despite being one of the smaller cats of the pride, he was nonetheless menacing as his massive claws swiped through the air in their direction, and it was clear that his powerful jaws could easily crush through their limbs. Eve's flesh trembled as she struggled to suppress the screams resounding within her. She dug her fingernails deep into Adam's skin.

There came a call from the pack that caused them and the cat to look across the plain. It appeared as though the feral beasts had satisfied their hunger and were moving on to return to their den, dragging the remainders of the carcasses with them for later feeding. The cat paced once more at the foot of the tree, stopping frequently to look toward the pack then back up at the two of them. After several moments of consideration, he turned away and ran off to follow his kin.

They remained motionless for a long while after the beast's departure, unable to release the tight grip they had upon the branches and on each other. The surge of blood and adrenaline continued to course furiously within them, yet they were unable to disperse the current of this internal storm, and this caused their muscles to remain locked in tension for long after the danger had gone.

When at last her shock and fear subsided, Eve's emotions were released in a stream of tears. Adam tried to subdue his own wave of emotions and give comfort to Eve, yet could not keep his own voice from trembling as he said, "The first of the evening stars will not be long in coming. We must hasten back to our place of rest and make preparations for sleep."

They made their way down the tree and back through the forest as quickly and as quietly as they were able. Being so unnerved and shaken by their experience with one of the beasts that hunts by day, they were of no desire to draw the attention of those which prowl in the darkness of the night.

The air had become heavy and thick. So much so that the moisture that hung in the atmosphere reflected the verdure of the plants, causing the air itself to appear a misty, dewy green. There was a quality of stillness and expectation in the air, marked by an imminence that was nearly as tangible as the damp stickiness it left on their flesh.

When they arrived at their sleeping space, they found that their simple shelter was no more. A few of the leaves and branches remained scattered about, though most were not to be found. Likely they had been taken to be used as nesting or shelter for the animals. Once again Adam created a small dwelling from newly gathered leaves and branches which he leaned against the large trunk of the tree. They had not eaten since early morning, though they both found that their hunger was only slight, as their fearful experience had left their stomachs knotted. Eve ate only a few of the olives and figs she and Adam had gathered along their way, then found herself yearning to succumb to the sweet escape of sleep.

She seemed better able to cope with the sounds of the night, or perhaps it was just that she was too exhausted to expend the same energy on vigilance as the night before. Adam had told her he would keep watch over her again and he would sleep in the morning. Thus, it was from a sound slumber that she was suddenly thrust awake by the first flash of light and the thundering of the sky.

Breathlessly she whispered, "Is it God?"

"I do not know for certain, but I do not believe so. I do not sense His coming as I did on that day."

"Nor do I, yet I do not understand what is happening."

They emerged from their shelter and there came another deafening crack that preceded more of the rumbling vibrations that coursed through the ether. It was still the time of darkness, but there were moments when the sky flashed into sudden eerie illumination and bolts of electric current severed the blackness of the night.

Drops of water began falling down on them from above. The droplets struck gently upon their skin at first, but then began to beat down faster and harder. Soon Eve and Adam were being furiously pelted by the water raining down upon them, and both stood shivering from the cold and the wet. The percussion of the rain upon the leaves became nearly as deafening as the blasts of thunder that exploded throughout the sky. They crawled back under their shelter of leaves, thinking it would help. But the fierce wind that had come to accompany the rain and thunder proved this act to be futile. The shelter collapsed and Adam tried to yell something to Eve, but his words were lost amid the thunder, the rain, and the wind. He then motioned for her to grab one of the larger leaves and hold it above her head, just as he was doing. They both tried to crouch low to the ground in order to expose as little of themselves as possible to the onslaught. Their feet began to sink into the thickening muck of the saturated ground. And as the mud started to slide downhill with the sloping of the ground, Eve slipped and fell. Adam grabbed her and pulled her back up. Quickly, he collected more large leaves and laid them out for them to kneel upon. Eve's muscles would tense and contract with a sudden jolt at each explosive burst of thunder that shook through her body. She squeezed her eyes tightly shut against the frightful sight of the lightning, but could not shut out her fears.

Even after the storm's initial intensity of roaring thunder and lightning had subsided, the rain remained hard and steady throughout most of the long night, seeming as if it would never end. As she and Adam continued to struggle against the mud and the cold rain, Eve could not keep her mind from reflecting on the contrast of the days she suffered the brutality of the arid emptiness of the desert, and how she had despaired that it would never come to an end. So many times she had prayed for just one drop of water to help her survive. She felt mocked by the disparity of what she had prayed for and what she had been given. Thoughts of an eternal deluge drowned her heart in dread throughout the loathsome night.

Chapter 14

Near dawn, the storm had diminished to random, pattering drops as the clouds began to break apart and slowly dissipate. The few wisps of clouds that did remain glowed in ribbons of soft pink and lavender hues, illuminated by the rising sun. The gusting winds had been replaced by a gentle breeze that carried upon it the bright and lively songs of the birds.

It was not only the birds that seemed to feel a renewed energy following the storm. There was an air of eager activity all around as the small ground animals were busy finding an abundance of food in the form of worms and grubs which had surfaced in the mud.

Despite all of the plant debris that had been blown down, the trees and bushes appeared fresh and lush, emanating a renewed vitality and emitting a younger shade of green. The allure of this vibrancy was so potent that it compelled Eve to touch her hand along the soft, serrated edges of the ferns and the feathery leaves of the flowering acacia so she could feel the life within them as she and Adam gathered their morning food.

Eve paused as she noticed an immense spider's web that hung suspended across a wide space between two giant sycamores. The sun's light caused the delicate silken threads to sparkle, and Eve wondered if it was newly spun, or if it had somehow withstood the storm. She was amazed at either possibility, as one meant that such an intricate and expansive weaving had been accomplished in the short time since the rain and wind had stopped, and the alternative would mean that it was tremendously strong and resilient despite its fragile appearance. She felt that she, too, was strong and resilient to have survived not only this storm, but also the desolation, fear and vulnerability she had felt since leaving Eden. Hope and a sense of lightness had replaced fear and despair.

As she was immersed in this new happiness, Adam, who was walking along behind her suddenly stopped and grasped her by the wrist, causing her to whirl around and face him. He was smiling, almost laughing at her as he asked, "What is that you're doing?"

"What do you mean?"

"There is a sound you are making that reminds me of the songs of birds, though it gladdens me more deeply than any cooing or whistling I have ever heard," he told her.

Eve had not been aware that she had given voice to her feelings of joy, and that she had been making a soft and melodic humming sound as they walked. Adam remained standing before her, but he was no longer smiling. Instead, he looked solemnly into her eyes. "I rejoice in each day, even throughout our days of agony in the desert, that I made the choice to eat the Fruit with you. I would suffer a thousand desert suns to hear these lovely sounds that you now make."

Hearing this made Eve happier still, but at first she was hesitant to continue humming and singing, as she had now become very self-conscious. As they continued on, however, she resumed giving voice to her happiness, as it was too natural to contain or repress.

After they returned to the place they had been sleeping, or rather had tried to sleep, the past few nights, they ate, and then Eve went to search for the coverings she had woven for them the day before. She had not had a chance to show them to Adam then, but had thought to place them beneath some stones to keep the animals from making off with them. This, however, had done little to protect them from the rain and the subsequent mud, which had left them in ruin. She would have to begin anew.

While she remained at their sleeping site for this purpose, Adam had decided to go deeper into the forest and ascend the heights of the trees to survey the land in order to better know their surroundings. He told Eve to remain wary of all of the noises around her, and to be vigilant to the behavior of the smaller animals, as their actions could portend any threat or approaching danger. Eve assured him that she would be fine and that she could easily climb up the branches of one of the trees that edged the small clearing if she became threatened.

When Adam had gone, Eve felt a kind of thrill in her belly that accompanied finding herself alone. It was a feeling of excitement and anticipation of the unknown rather than of fear. And though the sounds of the birds and the wind remained the same after Adam left, she felt a strange sense of quiet and solitude in the atmosphere around her.

As she began the work of gathering and weaving, however, the original thrill she had felt gradually subsided as she became more focused on her task. The hours of her day passed without event, and she completed her weaving before Adam returned. Once she was no longer occupied, she was surprised when she noticed just how much time had actually gone by, as the sun had moved from the eastern sky to the far west. She began to wonder as to Adam's safety and hoped he would return soon.

The longer she waited, the more restless she grew. She paced about the perimeter of the area as she struggled against an urge to try to go find him, though she knew that it would be foolish as she did not know for certain which direction would lead her to him. Still, as she walked, the space she moved in became wider and wider as she expanded the limits of her steps. Her resolve to heed Adam's warnings and confine herself within the small clearing was fading. She felt herself being drawn into venturing further into the thick of the trees. Though finding Adam was her foremost concern, she could not deny that she was also drawn by the allure of exploring within the forest.

Just as she had made up her mind to follow her desire and enter into the forest, Adam came into view and called to her. He approached her wearing a look of admonishment and spoke to her in a severe tone.

"What is it that you were planning on doing?"

Eve held his gaze and said nothing. Though she was guilty of nearly defying their agreement, she did not feel entirely sorry for her actions. She even felt somewhat justified in wanting to explore further, especially after being left on her own for so long.

Adam recognized by her silence that she would not apologize for her actions. He knew how strongly her heart pulled her to know and experience everything around her. He found this to be one of the most beautiful things about Eve, yet he could not allow her to be careless and put herself in danger. Thus, he remained unyielding in his stern reproach.

"I will not push you for an explanation, as I already understand your reasons. But do not undertake to stray into the wild alone and undefended again or I will become very angry with you. I know that you are both strong and clever, yet it is not acceptable for you to take such risks. This will not happen again."

Eve was about to argue against him that he had gone into the wild alone, and to make him explain how it was different for him than for her. But she stopped herself. She reflected on how he stayed awake to watch over her during the night when the nocturnal predators could be heard all around them. She remembered, too the way he had held her protectively in his arms when they had felt the curses of God befall them, and how safe and cared for those things had made her feel. She knew that Adam did not think her weak or frail, but it was simply who he was, as a man who loved and valued her, which made him want to defend her against harm. Instead of being offended or angry, she found herself delighting in the way it made her feel to be so cherished. She moved close to embrace him, wanting to yield to the pleasure of being wrapped within the strength of his body. Though Adam had not expected this, nor did he quite understand why she did it, he welcomed her touch as it dissolved away the tension between them.

Eve pulled away after a few moments. She was suddenly filled with excitement to show him the garments she had made for them. She explained how she had intertwined the sinuous fibers, weaving them in such a way that had created a strength and resilience that was far greater than that of the quickly made coverings they had in Eden. Adam wrapped it around his body. He was quiet in thought for many moments before he finally looked at Eve and spoke.

"What you have done is very good. It has given me the idea to build a stronger and more lasting shelter. We shall twine together fibrous plants to make walls to guard us from the beasts and a roof to shield us from the rains."

Excitedly, they began to gather various tall grasses, splicing them into thin threads which could be used to bind stems and vines together.

But they had not realized how immense an undertaking this would prove to be. Hours of labor turned into days, and they soon began to grow tired and disheartened by their efforts. Much of their initial rendering did not hold, becoming dry and brittle and snapping apart at the tension used in the weaving. They had tried working with many different types of plants when at last Adam discovered that the sedges and rushes that grew within the thick and swampy marshes did not grow brittle as easily as the river reeds, and would provide the greatest pliancy and water resistance for their shelter.

Even with the more workable marsh rushes, their task was not easy. Their hands became calloused and cramped from the continual weaving and the effort it required to create the adequate tension in the fibers.

During this time, both Adam and Eve had a growing awareness of a hunger within their bellies that they had not known before. The fruits and seeds which they had thus far lived on no longer seemed to fully satisfy or nourish them as in Eden.

Nor was their strength and energy as it had been in the Garden, and after the exertion each day of laboring to build their shelter they often went to sleep with aching stomachs, though at first neither of them spoke aloud of their discomfort and fatigue.

Each night that their shelter had yet to be completed, Eve had dreams filled with images of vicious beasts, violent storms, and the feeling of being vulnerable to some dark, lurking threat that seemed to be lying in wait for her. And so, she was filled with a great relief when at last the day came when she and Adam had completed weaving the walls of the hut and it was ready to be fortified. Adam added clay and mud mixed with dried grasses to strengthen and seal the seams where the walls were joined. They used long vines slung over the branches of the tree next to their shelter to aid them in hoisting up the thatched roof.

They rejoiced in the completion of their work and went together to the river to wash the dried mud and sweat from their skin. The water soothed their muscles from the pains of their long days of labor. They laughed and played in the cool water as they had in the carefree days before their exile.

As the sun disappeared below the horizon, they returned to the hut, garnering fruits and seeds along the way. They entered the shelter and sat upon the floor of palm leaves they had spread across the ground to make a soft place for them to sleep. When they had finished eating, Eve decided to speak of the hunger that lingered.

"I do not understand why even after I have eaten all that I can, I find my appetite has not been truly sated. I am not content, and I hunger for something more. My body yearns for some greater sustenance."

"It is this way for me as well," Adam answered. "Every night I am awakened by an emptiness, and I feel that my strength is lessening."

They began to question if they, too, could hunt and eat flesh as the predators did. They could not deny the lustful hunger they had felt at the sight of the great cats devouring the meat off of their prey. The land offered so much, yet their bellies seemed to crave something more.

They said nothing further, as neither of them relished the thought of eating flesh, and thus, it seemed there was nothing they could do but to accept their hunger. And despite the pangs of discomfort in their stomachs, they were both deeply grateful to be lying down to sleep within the safety they felt inside their new walls.

Eve's dreams of predators and storms were over. That night she had a different kind of dream. She was watching herself as if from above, walking through a vast field. It was not a meadow of flowers, as she had seen many times both here and in Eden. Nor was it a clearing or pasture as those in which the animals grazed. This field was unlike any she had ever seen. It was filled with grain. Not grain growing random and wild, but in cultivated rows. She walked between the rows, sweeping her hands across the tops of the stalks of wheat, causing the seeds to fall to the dirt. Some of these became buried in the ground beneath her feet, where they instantly sprouted anew. She bent to gather a few kernels that had not been buried. Even in the dream, her belly ached from hunger as it did in her waking hours, and she put the kernels into her mouth and tried to chew them to satisfy the aching, but the hulls were too hard and she had to spit them back upon the soil. Ahead of her, she saw a young calf walking between the rows. As its wide body moved along the wheat stalks, it too caused the grains to fall upon the earth. She moved up close behind the beast and saw that its hooves had crushed the kernels to a fine dust. She gathered this powdered grain into her hands and held it high up above her head, as if raising it to the sun. She could feel it grow warm and change its form, and she lowered her hands to see what had happened. It was no longer mere dust, but had been formed into a flat cake. She inhaled its sweet, warm scent, then broke this cake of bread in two, giving up half as an offering of gratitude, and the other half she ate. She began laughing.

"Eve, what is it?"

She opened her eyes as Adam asked again, "Eve, what is it? Are you all right? What happened?"

She looked up at him and smiled. He had woken her up often this way recently, worried about the troubled dreams he knew she had been having, wanting to stop the wild muttering and thrashing that had often intruded upon her sleep. She realized that he must have mistaken her laughter for crying.

"It was not one of those dreams," she said. "I have had a vision that will help us."

Adam interrupted before she could continue. "I have dreamed as well," he said. "My head was filled throughout the night with the echo of God's voice repeating the curse that I shall toil in the dirt and struggle for sustenance. I desperately implored God to tell me what it is that I am meant to do, but it was in vain, and my pleas remained unanswered. I fear that this curse is the cause of our hunger, but neither in my dream nor in the light of awakening do I see what can be done."

Eve stared at him, barely able to believe what seemed to have occurred. Her voice trembled as she began telling Adam what she had envisioned in her own dream. They were both confounded by the strangeness in the connection of their dreaming. The more they considered it and talked about the meaning, however, the more their astonishment evolved into hope, as it grew ever clearer to them what was to be done. Adam had often seen the wheat grain that Eve had dreamt of, as well as others, such as millet, oat and barley, but had known that the casings were too hard for them to eat directly off the stalk as some of the animals did. Yet somehow Eve's dream made sense to him, and he began planning how to cultivate the earth and sow the seeds which would feed and nourish them. They would have bread and grains to eat, and the hunger they felt would at last be nourished.

The next morning, Adam and Eve searched for the places where they knew the grains to grow wild, though only in sparse clusters. Adam had decided to harvest only what he thought was needed to begin his planting, taking care not to strip the stalks completely, as this was food for many of the animals. He also thought it prudent to leave plenty growing wild in case he was not successful in planting, and needed to gather more and start again. They folded the seeds carefully inside large leaves, and carried them back to their hut.

"Where will you sow the grains?" Eve asked him.

"I have seen a stretch of land not far from here, near the place where the river bends toward the east. There the soil is rich and dark, and though no large trees reside within this wide area, there is a profusion of brush and shrub that would need to be cleared before the earth would be ready for sowing."

Day after day Adam labored throughout the long hours of sunlight to prepare the earth for planting. He had walked the river's bank to gather stones to give aid to his labors. He chose only those which were keen-edged, though of various sizes to lend themselves to a variety of uses.

At first Adam worked on bended knees, holding the stone tools in his hands to turn the soil and dig to the roots of the brush and thistles. The hardship of his chore was further augmented by thick clods of clay which needed to be broken up. After days of laboring in this way, his hands had become blistered, bloodied and cramped, his legs were cut and scraped from the spiny thorns, and his back ached and was becoming bent. He thought he would need to give up his efforts until he came upon the idea to lash the stones to the ends of thick branches, which brought grea ease to his pains by allowing him to stand as he worked and to change the way he gripped with his hands.

And though the land did not give itself up easily to him, and every effort was met with resistance, the day finally came when Adam judged the earth to be prepared for sowing. He cut rows along the dirt and dropped the seeds within the furrowed trenches. He then swept the dirt over them, using a long leafy branch. Finally, just as he had done around the area of their hut, Adam surrounded the planted field with barbed vines strung between stakes to deter the beasts.

The sun was giving way to the evening as he finished lashing the last of the vines, and Eve beckoned him to come eat with her and rest from his labors.

Chapter 15

In the days that followed, Adam tended his fields and was careful to remove any weed or thorn that arose before it could leech the precious water and nutrients needed for his seeds. There were occasional gentle rains which fell to give drink to the sprouts which had at last begun to emerge through the dirt. Eve had thought to weave baskets from the same marsh reeds that they had used for their hut, and Adam used these to carry water from the river to keep the vulnerable shoots from wilting during the hot days between the rains.

Though Eve worked in many small ways to help Adam with his labors, it was he who tended to the strenuous tasks of working in his field and also to the frequent reparation that their shelter required to ensure its endurance against the ravages of wind, rain, and the small scavengers and insects that continually gnawed away at the reeds. Thus, at the twilight of each day it more often came to be that Adam's fatigue would fell him to an early slumber, and Eve would find herself restless. She began to feel herself pulled by a desire to leave the hut and be outside to experience the mysteries of the nighttime. This desire was mixed with excitement and a lingering murmur of past fears. She recalled how vulnerable she had felt during the nights before they had come to live within the safety of their shelter, and she nearly scoffed at herself for now being drawn back out into the darkness.

But there was a difference now. Adam had found a new way to help deter the nighttime beasts. One day while he was sharpening pieces of flint into tools for tilling by scraping them against each other, the stones gave off hot sparks. They discovered that when these sparks met with dried twigs and leaves, they caused a hot burning flame which could illuminate the darkness. Adam had dug holes and planted stakes with burning torches into the ground near enough to the entrance of their hut to ward off the animals. Yet, he was careful not to allow the flames too close, lest they or their hut be in danger of burning. It had been a terrible lesson to them to learn of the pain the fiery heat could inflict. Though they had both suffered blisters and burns on their skin during their days beneath the desert sun, the powerful intensity of the flames was such that a mere moment of contact with it could cause more pain and damage to their flesh than all of their days in the desert.

It was the idea of possessing such a potent force that gave Eve the courage to follow her yearning and leave Adam as he lie sleeping. She fashioned a small torch, with one end dipped in oil and resin to feed and control the flame. And with the boldness afforded her by this torch, she entered into the night alone.

Though she hadn't consciously planned where she was going, once she began walking the direction she took seemed natural, as if she were being guided. There was a small pond that she had taken to bathing in each morning after Adam left for the field, and it was there that she soon found herself. It lay within a grassy clearing encircled by thick brush where clusters of lilacs, dogwood trees, and vines of honeysuckle grew. She had always thought the pond and its surroundings were pretty on her morning visits, but when she walked through the edge of the forest into the clearing she was struck by the vast transformation she found there. Whenever she had gone there during the day, she had taken little notice of the flowering trees and bushes. It had always been the brilliant hues of red, yellow and orange wildflowers, illuminated in the sunshine, that had filled her senses. It was the gentle scent of these that usually wafted upon the air.

But in the dusky twilight, everything within the clearing had become new and different. She gazed up in breathless wonder at the open sky above as it revealed the infinite expanse of the starlit heavens and the full and rising moon. Its ambient glow caused the white and blue clusters of flowers to almost shimmer with a silvery opalescent luster. Eve removed her garments and breathed in deeply, allowing the erotic sweet scents of the garden to wash over her. The heavily perfumed air suddenly overtook her with a swooning intoxication, causing a fluttering thrill in her stomach and making her heart beat excitedly. For a moment, she had difficulty steadying herself from the dizzying effect, yet she enjoyed giving herself over to its influence.

As she dipped her foot into the water, rippling the reflection of the moonlight, Eve felt as if she were infusing herself directly into the moon, becoming steeped within its glow. There was something in the dewy atmosphere of the evening air, the cool water on her skin, the evening song of the crickets, and the illuminated dance of the fireflies, that seemed to be a pure reflection of something within herself. All of these things, especially the moon, emanated an essence of femininity that seemed to draw from her, rather than cast upon her, a radiant sensuality. The experience was similar to how she felt when she connected sexually with Adam. But this was a sensual connection with herself. She found pleasure in the way the moon's light touched upon her glistening wet skin, emphasizing the curves of her flesh, and it was as if she was sharing a secret, one that could not be expressed in words, with the starlit heavens. She felt an awakening of both flesh and spirit, and it made her aware of some new kind of energy, a kinetic potential, building up within her.

The seduction of these feelings lured her to steal away from the hut, leaving Adam asleep and alone on many nights. Before she had begun these solitary excursions, she had often laid beside him in silence, gazing up through the small opening in the roof of their hut at the evening sky. But the way she saw that same sky when she was alone and immersed in the nighttime caused the heavens to take on a very different and exciting quality for her. She would look up at the limitless expanse and sense that she herself was just as infinite and boundless as the heavens.

Eve noticed that each night she returned to the pool, the moon had been gradually waning, until finally there came a night where she found herself beneath a dark and moonless sky, with only the distant stars and her small torch to illuminate her way. There had seemed to be a growing sense of purpose in returning to the water each night, and over the course of these nights her original anticipation had been changing into an expectant, almost restless, impatience. She felt relief, however, as she entered into the calm, quiet water.

When she had gone out far enough for the water to encircle her waist, she felt the tide of tension that had been building within her relax and release forth, and she became aware that something strange and unknown to her had just occurred beneath the surface. She placed her hand into the pool and reached down between her thighs. When she brought her hand back up she could tell, even in the dimness of the moonless night, that the dark crimson fluid upon her hand was her own blood.

A flood of emotions swelled within her, and at first she was very frightened. She had only seen blood when it was part of an animal's death or injury, or in small amounts from the damage the desert sun had caused to their blistered lips. She knew that it was vital for life, yet her initial sense of panic was fleeting. She did not feel pain or weakness. To the contrary, she almost immediately returned to feeling that same strong sense of her own beauty and sensuality that she always became rapt within when she came to the pool. Though she did not fully understand why this shedding of blood was happening, she recognized that this must be part of the secret; part of the silent mystery she had sensed that she shared with the moon and stars, the water, and the flowers that bloomed at night in her vespertine garden. It left a warm tingling feeling in her belly.

Later, when she returned to the hut, she kissed Adam gently on his forehead, then she laid down at a distance from him. She struggled against her desire to be near him and feel the reassuring warmth of his body. She thought that he would have even less understanding of what was happening to her than she did. She worried that he may fear it, and thus fear her.

She slept lightly and only intermittently, wanting to be sure she was up before Adam so she could go to the river and let the moving water cleanse her before he saw her. After she did this, she gathered food for them while Adam remained asleep in the early dawn.

When Adam arose, they ate together and Eve said nothing of what was happening within her body. She had decided to stay near the river so she could bathe throughout the day. Adam would be intent on his labors in his field and would not notice.

Eve continued in this way on the days that followed. Upon the fifth rising of the sun the bleeding subsided and finally ceased. During these days she had chosen only to bathe in the flowing water of the river and had not returned to the pond. It did not seem right to her to let her blood come forth into the calm pool. Now that it had ended, however, she longed to return to the quiet stillness and beauty of her secret place.

She experienced this same pattern of the ebb and flow of emotions and the shedding of blood many times. She would feel her energy amplify and surge into fullness as she would gaze up each night at the waxing moon, its own light and energy also expanding in a synchronous rhythm. Then after reaching fullness, the moon would once again begin to wane, just as her energy would gently begin to ebb and subside. These cycles always culminated in the release of blood and would leave her with the discordant feeling of a potential unfulfilled and a vague, unexplainable sadness of a promise unmet. Eve often wept as the river water flowed past her hips and thighs, carrying with it some part of herself she felt was lost. Sometimes her tears stemmed from the frustration she felt with Adam for his inability to understand these tides of emotion, even though she herself did not fully comprehend the feelings of loss and loneliness that her blood carried with it.

Ever since the days of sowing, Adam had remained almost continually absorbed with tending the plants, which had finally matured and become ready for the harvest. Eve had been occupied in recent days weaving new baskets in preparation for the collection of the grain. The season had twice changed since the sowing of the land, with the air growing cooler and the moon appearing earlier each night in the twilight sky.

On the night before the harvest, Adam was still out in his field as a yellow-orange moon arose, appearing to loom closer and larger, and shining with a brilliance unlike any they had seen before. Eve felt the pull of this moon more strongly than ever. But on this night it wasn't the allure of venturing out alone that she felt. She had been missing Adam more and more during their long days of separation. She was filled with excitement at the promise of tomorrow's harvest, but even more so because Adam would be able to spend more of his time with her again.

Some days she had even found herself resenting the fields for taking Adam away from her, even though she knew that his labors were for the benefit of both of them. His work left him fatigued and needing sleep. And even in the time they spent together eating before he slept, he was often quiet, contemplating how to overcome the many challenges he faced in tending to the field. But now, she thought, Adam could rest from his toil, and she would refrain from going out alone if it meant sharing more time with him. She had been feeling a growing sense of longing in her heart when she was in her moonlit garden, wishing that Adam was there with her, looking upon her, and seeing how beautiful and luminous she was beneath the glow of the heavens.

As she looked up at this immense and magnificent moon, she had the impression that it was converging upon her, that it would imminently consume her. It caused her to want Adam even more so it could consume them both in the rapture of its glow. Eve's heart beat with an urgent lust, fueled by the spell cast upon her senses from the fulgent, evocative moon, as well as the erotic influence of estrus flowing within her. As she came upon the field, she could see the form of his body silhouetted against the twilight sky, and the fire within her stirred even hotter. When she approached Adam he was intent on examining a handful of grains. He briefly greeted her, barely looking up, and proceeded to voice his worries about the harvest. He spoke of his hope that he had done everything right to ensure they would have enough.

This was not the reception she had expected, and as he continued talking only about the crops, Eve felt the fire of her longing transform almost instantly to a hot rage. She demanded that Adam look at her, and she raised her voice, screaming out her words, fierce and unrestrained.

"How dare you to treat me thus! You have long neglected and forsaken me for these fields! You think only of how to best work the soil and how to care for your precious crops! Have you forgotten how to care for *me?* You have become ignorant of my needs as your friend and as your wife, denying me your affection and your intimacy! It has been long since you have hearkened to me, and I have suffered in your absence! I have been wronged by your actions and your apathy towards me! You cause me to be envious of the dirt! Your mind dwells on it, your hands touch it, and your eyes look upon it day after day to ensure it is good enough for your crops to flourish! You no longer think of me, or touch me, or look upon me to see if I am flourishing or if I am suffering!"

Bewilderment washed over Adam. This furious outcry was beyond his comprehension and had taken him completely unaware. He was about to offer an apology, though he did not quite know for what, when Eve suddenly grasped the back of his neck and pulled his mouth to hers. Her anger with him became aggression. Hunger and lust overtook her and she kissed him hard as she drew him down with her upon the rich black soil of the field. She wrapped her legs around his body, asserting her desire upon him. Her hands gripped at his shoulders and her nails dug deeply into his skin. He responded with an increased intensity and force in the motions of his body. As he overtook her, Eve softened to him, fully abandoning herself to the primal influence of the rich earthy musk and the salty sweet taste of Adam's skin. At last, this is what she wanted, what she needed...

*   *   *

Though Eve's fervor had calmed as she lay breathless upon the earth, wrapped in the afterglow of the experience, the truth remained that their act had been initiated in a torrent of aggression and jealousy, and thus the seed of their act was sown.

Chapter 16

Another change of season had come shortly after the harvest and had brought with it unexpected difficulties. Adam realized that the ground could not be immediately re-tilled as the cool rains had become more steady and frequent, replacing the usual light and warmth of the sun, and the nights had grown longer and colder. He had undertaken to dig a pit in the floor of their shelter, lining it with sand and stones so they could keep a fire burning within it for warmth and to bake their bread. Adam had also taken to cleaning and paring the hides of any recently slain animals that he came upon, using the skins as cloaks against the evening cold throughout the long season of dormancy.

By the time the days once again began to lengthen and the sun's warmth dissipated the last of the frost from the ground, the stores of grain were nearly depleted, and much of what had been harvested all those months ago had spoiled early on. They had since learned to keep the grain in more tightly woven baskets fortified with dried mud and clay, and to cover them to help deter the rodents and at least some of the insects.

Throughout this time, Eve's belly had been growing big with child. Though she had felt the change come upon her soon after the harvest, she had not immediately known what it meant. She was frequently afflicted with waves of nausea, and her patterns of appetite had drastically changed. Then, on the night of the next new moon, when the expected release of life's fluid from her body did not come, she began to understand. This sacred blood was fulfilling its purpose, to nurture and propagate new life. Even before her belly had begun to effloresce, she was aware that the flesh below her navel, usually soft, had become firm and taught. She had observed the way this change had happened in the female animals in the time leading up to the birth of their young, and she knew that she, too, would give birth, but did not know when. She had seen how the time of growth within the mother's body varied among the different species. She thought that her time would be similar to that of the apes she had known in Eden, but she had not been in Eden long enough to witness the entire length of their gestation.

As the child within her grew, Eve's thoughts frequently dwelled upon her memories of watching the primates that she had felt such a kindred connection with. She had seen no apes living in this region of land, yet she would not allow herself to think that they dwelled only within the Garden. She liked to imagine that if she and Adam had gone in a different direction they may have come upon a land not only inhabited by apes, but also would have found many of the other species of animals, plants, and fruits that they had known in Eden but had not seen here.

In Eden, she had been fascinated by how the ape mothers tended to their young. The infants would cling to the mother, dependent for their food and care, dependent for survival. Eve had witnessed how those mothers, who often engaged in brutal conflicts with each other, and who could fiercely defend themselves and their offspring from predators, were also capable of extreme gentility and tenderness toward their young, and appeared to take great care in nurturing and teaching them. The young seemed to remain with their mothers for much longer than the offspring of other creatures did.

Eve tried to quell the fears that often welled up inside her regarding the unknown child within her womb with thoughts of having seen how those primates, who were similar to her and Adam in so many ways, appeared instinctively to know how to care for their young and keep them safe. Yet, it occurred to her that perhaps it was not entirely instinct for them, as the ape mothers were once the young and they had had the benefit of learning these things from the experience of their own mothers. Eve had no mother to teach and guide her. In this, she envied the apes. She had a growing impression of missing something by not having another woman to learn from. Eve wondered what it would be like to have her own mother; someone who could understand how she had felt when she first began her moon cycles; someone who had gone through the same changes and experienced the same stirring of emotions; someone to calm her fears about delivering this child from her flesh unto the world. She loved Adam, yet only another woman would have been able to fill this particular longing.

But any feelings of lacking or uncertainty were eclipsed by the joy she found in the profound gift she had been given. She was experiencing the creation of life within her own flesh and she could sense the sublime and the miraculous in this. It mattered not that she could not comprehend that the continual fusing and splitting of particles echoed the same phenomenal cosmic events from which the entire universe had been born, or that the growth of this child within her womb mirrored the transitions and patterns of evolution, developing in response to what the world would require for survival, shifting from a state of utter dependence and safety to one of autonomy and strength in order to meet the demands of the unknown.

The Garden had been as a womb for Adam and herself. They had needed to grow and mature, just as the child within her, in order to face what the world outside of Eden's protective barriers would demand of them.

*   *   *

Many days and many moons had come and gone. The new seeds that had been planted within the earth in the early spring had sprouted and grown tall enough for Adam to be sure of their viability and strength. Though he continued to tend to the field each day, he took care to return to the hut and see to Eve as often as he could. He brought fresh water to her to help keep her cool now that the days had grown long and hot, causing Eve to become easily flushed with exhaustion. She confined her activity to the early mornings and the evenings, resting the remainder of the day so she could reserve her energy.

Eve loved the sensation of the child's increasing movement within her. It seemed to simultaneously emphasize how connected she was to this being, yet also how separate and individual this life was from her own. She was beginning to sense that the time of birth was nearing. There had been a shift in the way she carried the child, allowing her breath to flow more freely than it had for several weeks, and with this had also come a pervading sense of calm and internal quieting of Eve's mind and spirit. Her energy was focused on readying herself for what was to come. She had asked Adam to prepare additional pelts to swaddle the newborn in, and they had both taken extra care to see to any mending of the hut that needed to be done. They wanted to ensure it would be resilient and strong enough to protect the fragile new life which soon would dwell within its walls. Despite these acts of preparing themselves for the coming of their child, Eve continued to experience moments where her mind could barely conceive the reality of this strange and remarkable experience.

Chapter 17

Eve's cries of pain severed the quiet of the night and echoed through the trees as her muscles gripped and constricted, bearing down in response as she struggled to regain control of her breath. The first contractions had woken her in the midst of the darkest hours. It had started as a sensation of pressure that came and passed erratically, and then a surge of fluid flowed forth from her body. The pressure changed and intensified, and Eve was soon engulfed within the throes of grueling pains which seized upon her with increasing regularity. Each time the torment subsided she was left fatigued and unable to take comfort in the brief reprieve, for she knew that it would not be long before the pain overtook her once again. She could not find lasting ease through any movement, nor could she comfortably remain still. She paced the floor of the hut, febrile and panting while Adam looked upon her, feeling a mix of fear and helplessness. Suddenly Eve's breath became quick and shallow once more, and in between gasps she cried out,

"I am being torn apart! I need to be at the water! Take me to the water now! I cannot breathe in here!"

Then, just as Eve was about to collapse to the ground, Adam quickly lunged forward and caught her. He supported her as he began walking her toward the river.

Her voice scarcely more than a raspy whisper, she managed to say "No, not the river. The pool in the clearing."

Adam got her to the small pond as quickly as he could and rested her upon the soft grass at the water's edge just as the next wave of contractions began, lasting longer and bringing even greater agony than the others. When the surge finally subsided, Eve sat on the bank with her feet immersed, and with great effort she dipped her cupped hands into the water and poured it over her head to cool her face and rinse off the sweat that had matted down her hair.

Adam felt desperate to help ease her burden. Seeing her afflicted with such suffering and distress was torture for him. He felt powerless and weak, but even more, he was afraid. He did not know how much more her body or her spirit could take. She looked so exhausted and pale.

Eve's words broke through Adam's worry. "Help me into the water."

He was alarmed by her request. "But you cannot go into it! What if the baby begins to come?"

Her voice was hoarse and her throat nearly raw as she said, "Please do not contest this. I need to be in the water… and I need you there with me!"

Adam did as she bid him, though it frightened him greatly. They stood within the shallows where the water rose just to Eve's hips, and soon there came a moment where all fell silent and still as Adam gazed into Eve's eyes and saw that they held a calm clarity. It was as if the entire world held its breath in an expectant hush, as in the seconds just before the dawning sun breaches the horizon.

Barely audible, Eve whispered, "It is time."

The moment of tranquility suddenly broke as Eve's flesh became once again locked in tension. She wailed as her hands clutched onto Adam's arms, pulling them down into the water. Her muscles compressed and contracted as she continued to scream out in agony. All she could think was, "I'm dying. God has taken his final vengeance and this is how I shall die." She only wanted to know that the child had been born and delivered safely into Adam's hands. What happened to her afterward did not matter now. She struggled and pushed to bring her baby forth, fearing that her strength would not be great enough. She fought for every breath she took. Her consciousness began ebbing away as her weakened body grew lax and slipped down further into the water.

"Eve! Eve, you cannot stop! You need to push! The child's head is in my hands! You must continue to be strong and bring this child forth!"

Eve responded to the passionate desperation in Adam's voice, and with a will of energy beyond what she thought she possessed, she gave forth a final exertion of effort. Her flesh tore violently and blood poured forth from her. Adam thought she would lose too much for her life to be sustained. She had already become weak and frail from the strain, though she somehow continued to persevere and at last delivered the babe into Adam's hands.

The next several moments were filled with Adam's fervid actions to ensure that both Eve and the infant were safely out of the water. As Eve lie shivering upon the grass, Adam was bent down over the newborn, whose skin was a purplish-blue, and who did not appear to be breathing. Adam worked desperately to rouse the baby by rubbing and tapping gently upon its chest and back as he whispered frantic pleas to Heaven for the infant to breathe.

Eve's head started to clear and she could perceive that something was wrong. She looked toward Adam and the baby, and with a tremulous whisper she asked, "What is wrong? Adam, what is happening?"

She tried to sit up to see, but her head swooned and she dropped back down. She had become dehydrated and had lost too much blood.

Adam continued his efforts, and finally, there came a response. After several feeble sputtering noises the child gave out a loud, strong cry. It was a sound that would forever be imprinted upon Adam's heart. His own existence had suddenly become both nothing and everything all at once.

This tiny, fragile being that could be held within his hands was more important to him than his own life, yet his own life took on greater meaning and importance somehow because of it. He then looked upon Eve, whose flesh was the sacred vessel through which this child, his own son, had been born. He saw how radiantly beautiful she was, and knew that her flesh was the physical connection between the Divine Inspiration of Heaven and the manifestation of their love in the form of this beautiful boy. Tears brimmed in his eyes.

Adam placed the babe in Eve's arms and gathered them both up to carry them back to the hut. He wrapped them in the warm, soft animal skins he had prepared. He knew Eve needed fresh water, but it was difficult for him to think of leaving them. Eve could sense his hesitation and assured him that all would be fine while he was gone.

It was with great reservation that Adam finally departed after he had assisted Eve in getting comfortable, leaning her back upon a pile of furs for support with the baby nestled safely in her arms. Once alone, it was not long before the infant had rooted onto her breast. Eve gazed down upon this child sucking sweetly at her bosom, and she was rapt in the quiet intimacy between them. This tiny being was an innate part of herself. Looking at him, she could imagine him as a grown man, tall and strong. Perhaps he, like his father, would find joy in cultivating the land, and he, too, would grow to be brave and good. He would bring happiness unto them and fill them with pride at his achievements. He would fulfill the potential of the life he had been given.

But in the stillness of the moment, her hopeful visions began to give way to doubt and uncertainty. In the deepest corners of her heart there was the unsettling ache of the unknown. In truth, this child was as yet a stranger to her. She did not know what his desires and longings would be, nor the nature of his fears or the disposition of his character. She became fraught with the idea that he may not become all that she hoped. She worried that he may not always choose what is right, and that he may experience times of sadness and despair that she could not protect him from. She looked again into his eyes, and knew that both her hopes and her doubts would, for now, remain unanswered. Only with time would she come to know who this child was, and who he would grow to be.

Eve shook away these unsettling notions from her mind, feeling guilty at allowing anything other than the warm elation of holding her newborn child enter into her heart and her mind. She consoled herself with reassurances that any doubts she harbored were simply due to weakness, the loss of blood, and her need for water. As soon as Adam returned to her she would drink and be taken care of and with her needs allayed, all things would be right and good, just as they should be. Holding onto this belief, she slipped into sleep.

Chapter 18

Eve's flesh had healed from labor, and on the morning that marked the passing of one full cycle of the moon since the birth, she and Adam awakened early, and as their child remained in slumber they readied themselves for this anticipated day.

As they finished their morning meal, the baby began to stir among the pile of skins they slept upon. Eve picked him up and nurtured him at her breast before wending their way toward the pond. It was there, at the place of his birth, that the name of their son would be proclaimed unto him before God.

For Eve, there was another significance to this day. In giving birth she had experienced the wonder and the ecstasy of the Divine working through her flesh in the creation of a life. This had inspired a wave of new sentiments toward God, and brought to her heart a sense of a hallowed union between herself and her Creator. Any bitterness she had felt toward God for the hardships she and Adam had borne was now dissolved, and joy had taken root in its place.

When they arrived at the pond, she and Adam removed their garments and Eve unswaddled their baby. After lowering herself into the water she reached up to receive the baby from Adam. Then he, too, entered into the pool. Eve cradled the child in her arm as she gently poured water over him to cleanse him. She and Adam turned their eyes toward the heavens, and Adam said:

"We offer up a benediction of thanks to God for granting unto us the blessing of this beautiful son, who shall henceforth bear the name of 'Cain'."

Eve lowered the babe once more into the warm water, speaking softly and singing to him, calling him by his new name as she continued to bathe him. She felt as though with the coming of this child, her life would evermore be filled with unwavering happiness. She thought that she and Adam had finally been granted a reprieve from the trials which had plagued them in the past. They had shelter and fire, which helped keep them safe from storms and from predators. Adam had learned how to work the land to provide food for them. She had given birth to this healthy, vibrant child. It seemed right to give praise to God and to allow herself to feel content and secure.

*   *   *

The harvest of that second year had proven even more plentiful than their first. Adam had continued to gain a deeper understanding of the land and of the seeds which he sowed. Earlier in the planting season he had sought to cultivate seeds from not only the grains, but several other types of vegetation as well. He had even planted a grove of fruit-bearing trees. As he tended the soil and grew food for their sustenance he learned how to respond to the needs of the earth and of his crops.

Soon after Cain had been born, Eve had begun going to the fields with him cradled at her bosom. Sitting among the tall grasses and flowers which ran along the edge of the field, she would speak quietly to her son, describing to him the work that his father was doing, telling him that someday when he was grown that he, too, would create food from seed and soil.

Eve derived immense pleasure from being near to Adam as he labored, and it was exciting for her to see the way he used his body to work with the land. He had always appeared strong, but the way his form had changed in response to laboring in the fields had caused him to become even more desirable to her now than he ever had been in Eden. Eve realized that Adam would not have acquired these strengths if they had remained in the Garden, where all would have been provided for them. Adam would have been deprived of this experience, unable to feel the satisfaction and pride of accomplishment. He now emanated such a powerful sense of purpose and fulfillment which came from being part of the process of creating something living, and from nurturing his plants to help them grow and thrive. These things further deepened her feelings of respect and honor toward him. She felt a sensual connection between them whenever her hands would grind down the grain and knead bread from the wheat that Adam had grown.

The abundance of the harvest sustained them through the rains and chill of the months that followed. Cain was growing strong and robust, and by the time the soil was once again ready for its third season of tilling, Eve had to keep constant watch over him to prevent him from crawling into harm. He was incessantly in motion following wherever his curiosity led him. It was not long before he could easily stand on his own, and soon he was even able to walk without the need of his mother's hands for support.

It became increasingly difficult for Eve to finish any task without interruption, especially potentially dangerous ones, such as setting fire in the hearth to bake their bread, as she needed to be ever vigilant to Cain's needs and to his safety. And though she often sighed aloud whenever she had to suspend her own activities to tend to Cain, in her heart she savored how he needed her.

As the days grew longer and hotter Cain quickly went from walking to running, leaving Eve with a tinge of loss and longing to once again experience the tenderness of a baby at her breast. She tried to cradle Cain close to her as he lie sleeping, but it never lasted. His sleep was often fitful and he would unknowingly push her away and mutter complaints of agitation at being too hot and too crowded. So, sadly, she came to leave him be as he slept.

Adam's field yielded more bounty with each of the next three years of harvest, but then came a season unlike the others. Long had it been since any rain had fallen, or even since clouds had gathered to give the land reprieve from the sun's glare. Adam was growing ever more exhausted from the constant struggle to bring enough water to the plants to keep them alive. Many leaves and stalks had begun to blacken and fall to the dirt, becoming mere dust underfoot. Adam was frustrated, carrying a constant sense of dread in his heart. He spoke little at the end of the day, and when he did speak, he was often terse and impatient.

When Eve offered to help him bring water to the fields as she had often done before Cain was born, it only served to further anger and frustrate him. His tone was harsh when he answered her.

"It is *my* inherent duty to provide food for my family! If I fail in this, it shall be my own burden and shame to bear. It may be that God has chosen this time to fulfill the curse proclaimed unto me. If that is the truth of this, then there is nothing you could endeavor to do that would prevent the bane of His will from being fulfilled."

"But how could God inflict such despair into that which has given you so much joy and cause futility in your struggle and effort?"

Adam answered, "*What God giveth, God can taketh away.*"

These words echoed in Eve's mind and caused her to shudder, as if they portended a meaning far more grave than the destiny of the fields. Without knowing why, she was suddenly compelled to reach out to Cain and clutch him tightly to her bosom, feeling as if he could somehow be taken from her. Though he twisted and struggled in effort to return to his play, she did not release him from her protective embrace for a long time.

The days that followed seemed to stretch out in an endless stream of despair, and the strain was heavy on Adam. Both his body and spirit were becoming further drained with each passing day. But he would not cease in his efforts nor allow himself to succumb to his exhaustion. He had learned from Eve what it meant to follow through with your highest intent and act accordingly with your soul, even if death be the ultimate price. It was through working with his hands in the soil that he felt he had discovered his purpose on this earth. Growing food to nourish those he loved gave a sense of accordance and union between himself and the land, between himself and his family, and perhaps most of all between himself and God. For it was God that formed the earth, provided the first grains, and had given Adam his very life, including the capacity to perform this work of farming the land. If God now chose to take that from him, He would be taking something of value from Himself as well. Adam prayed to God not to forsake him and to help him with his burdens.

"Why, my God, do You not respond to my pleas? Why must You test my spirit and bring me discouragement and strife for my efforts?"

It seemed as though Adam's petitions were not heard, and the drought continued on until greater than half of the field had been ravaged and withered by the sun's desiccation. Adam's weariness only grew, and his resolve to persevere weakened. Though Eve had abided by Adam's wishes that she not help him in the fields, she yearned to offer herself to him in some way that would lessen the weight that he felt was his alone to carry. She had watched him all these days and had kept her silence, not wanting to force him to speak about his frustration and his increasing sense of hopelessness. She knew he felt that he had somehow failed her and failed himself. Eve saw the signs of his prolonged agony in the deepening lines of his face, his absence of appetite, and in his sallow and withdrawn countenance. She knew that Adam could not bear this strain for much longer and she searched desperately within her heart to discover some means to help him. She had remained in abeyance for too long and was now determined to do something.

After preparing yet another meal for him which he did not eat and then putting Cain to sleep, Eve lay down next to Adam, shrouded in the familiar heavy silence that had come to dominate their nights. She remained awake for many hours in contemplation of what she could possibly do that would help Adam without interfering in what he saw as his own yoke of responsibility. But eventually, despite her worry and distracted thoughts, sleep overtook her.

Within the realm of slumber, however, Eve's mind continued to dwell upon Adam's needs. And in the quiet language of dreams, when the senses are hushed and the mind can truly hearken to the wisdom of the heart, Eve received an answer.

The revelation of her dream began with the vision of a circle, or ring, suspended amidst utter blackness. It bore a palpable quality of cold rigidness, seeming unbendable and restricted. Then came a faint glimmer originating at its center. It was a gentle glow that expanded and evolved into a brilliantly pulsating orb of light that radiated a warm energy outward toward the perimeter of the ring. The source of light was in itself quite delicate and vulnerable, but the waves of heat it produced were potent enough to permeate the outer sphere, softening it and causing it to become more pliant, increasing its capacity for resilience and flexibility. With these qualities it grew ever stronger. No longer cold and brittle, the ring itself came to shine brightly with the same divine light that was born within its center. The outer ring acted as a fortress, providing protection to the inner core of light. The entire entity melded together and became as one, impenetrable and vibrant in its state of perfect completion.

The perspective of the vision widened and shifted so that the inner pulsating glow transformed into the image of a beating heart, and the outer ring came to resemble the form of a body. The flesh and bones were now the fortress, serving to protect the vulnerable heart. The body itself was strong, but completely dependent upon the heart to circulate the energy and the blood of life throughout it. It was the heart that generated the body's pulsing rhythm and vitality. Each aspect of the whole fulfilled its purpose, and each was equally dependent upon the other for survival.

The image faded away as Eve awoke from her dream and looked upon her beloved Adam. She recognized that he always acted in ways to protect her, and that a large part of his agony now was the fear of being unable to defend her from hunger and wanting. She also knew that he needed her now more than ever before to support him by giving to him the energy of her love. He needed to experience the essence of her, as a woman, to strengthen his own qualities as a man. He was her fortress and she was his heart.

She realized that as Adam had been immersed in his troubles, she had been absent to him by preoccupying herself in seeing only to the needs of Cain. She felt guilty for allowing the growing distance that had separated them from intimacy. She could see that she had been wrong in leaving Adam to suffer alone in his worries each night, and that just because he refused her help in the fields did not mean he did not need her. She had been neglectful of him, and of their connection as man and woman.

Though the sun had not yet risen, the darkness of night was gently ebbing away and the sky was lightening to a soft violet blue. Adam typically awoke with the light of the dawn, but on this day Eve roused him from sleep and awakened him with her desire. She laid her hand first upon his chest and held it there for a moment, feeling the strength and rhythm in the rising and falling of his breath before continuing to move her hand down along the line of his body. Through the gentle pressure of her touch she tried to convey the depth of her devotion to him. Adam's flesh responded to her touch and his eyes blinked open to behold the vision of Eve's dark and comely form upon him. She looked up at him and made a silent acknowledgement with the nod of her head toward Cain, who remained soundly sleeping. With unspoken consonance they quietly arose and took leave of the hut.

As soon as they stepped out into the dewy morning air, Adam took hold of Eve and bedded her down upon a patch of softly scented heather and clover that grew outside their door. With his hand beneath her head, Adam pulled Eve's face close to his. His mouth encompassed hers, biting and sucking the honeyed sweetness of her lips. Their passion for each other arose and heightened as their flesh became entwined and their souls fused. A wave of desire ascended within her, and she surrendered to it, relinquishing herself to Adam, giving all to him. As he received the intent of this offering, absorbing the healing nature of her love, he gave forth the manifest expression of his own virile energy, the sacred seed of life.

Eve had not realized until this moment how her own desire had been left unfulfilled. She was like the thirsty land and her sensuality had been left forsaken. But with the rushing waves of excitement and the release of love's sweet amrita from her flesh, her feminine soul had been roused from slumber. Her senses awakened to everything that was encompassed within this moment; the sound of the wind whispering its secrets to the leaves, the feel of the breeze as it moved across her skin the richness of the soft earth as she dug her fingers into the ground, grasping handful of dirt and clover in the heat of her ecstasy; the sighs of their passion merging with the sounds of the distant rushing river; the birds singing their sweet morningsong. All that was around them had become a part of the experience of their love.

Eve lingered within the pleasure of Adam's arms enfolded around her as the sun breached the horizon and cast the world in a soft pink glow that shone upon her dark hair and lit upon the soft curves of her body. Adam put his hand beneath her chin and lifted her face to his. Eve felt deeply pleased to see the calm serenity of his expression, which held a peacefulness that had been absent far too long.

"I have been encumbered by despair," he told her. "I have felt alone and lost in hopelessness. It is you who has brought my spirit back to life. Your love has healed my desolation, and I have felt my own salvation come upon me through the warmth of your flesh. Because of you, this is the first morning in so very long that I have not awoken to a feeling of dread, heavy as a stone, laden upon me. Instead, my waking thoughts were of love and of hope. I feel on the dawning of this new day that my strength and determination have been re-alighted and I am delivered from the weight of my troubles. I will not abandon my efforts, and shall work to preserve what I can of the crops. Whatever is able to be spared is surely saved by the strength of your love."

As he kissed her, Eve experienced a sudden 'knowing' in her heart that something hallowed and sublime had befallen them on this morning. The spark of a new life had been kindled within her belly.

*   *   *

The solace of their embrace was broken by the waking cries of Cain from inside the hut. They both quickly arose to tend to the duties of the day that demanded their attention. Adam went to his fields and Eve went to their child.

Chapter 19

Though it had still been many days before the rains came, the thunderclouds at last had gathered to darken the skies and release their gift upon the thirsty land, anointing the soil with each drop that fell. Adam had proven himself strong and had persevered until then, and it came to be that joy entered into both Adam and Eve's hearts, as not only had enough of the harvest been spared to sustain them, but soon after the rain had come Eve began to feel the quickening of life that swelled within her.

Waves of exhilaration would cause her to become flushed, at times even breathless, with euphoria. The changes taking place within her flesh felt just as much a sacred mystery as when she had carried Cain. Part of the same mystery of creation that gave rise to the stars and the seas was once again occurring within her womb. This time she felt freer to relax into the wonder and happiness of the experience without the worry and fear of the unknown.

Cain was yet too young to comprehend the reason for the changes in his mother, though he gladly reaped the benefits of her elated happiness. Eve doted on him increasingly. Her feelings of love and expectancy toward the child growing within her womb were often outwardly expressed through her indulgences upon Cain. She would spend many hours teaching him new things and encouraging him to be unafraid of challenges, praising him highly for any new accomplishment. She tried to foster his sense of independence and autonomy by giving him more and more complicated chores. She also began to allow him to play alone within the hut while she would work at grinding wheat just outside the door. She would repeatedly tell him how proud she was that he was so big and strong to be able to do these things on his own. Cain could not have known that she was preparing him to rely on her less, as would be necessary once the new child was born. He simply reveled in her praise and attention.

Adam, too, felt better able to savor this time of waiting for the birth, the weight of his own anxieties allayed by the familiarity of what was happening to Eve. He looked with a deepening love upon her ripening flesh, the sensual fullness of her breasts, and the radiance that shone from her deep brown eyes. He found a beautiful allure in the rounded curves of her body that reflected the essence of complete feminine purity and sacredness. Her pregnant flesh was the embodiment of love in all of its forms.

Adam had come to realize that he had been expending a great amount of energy and time in worrying about their future. He had learned through the drought that losing himself to these cares had not served him. Eve's support, along with his own resolve to endure, were what had carried him through and allowed him to reap the harvest. In his heart, Adam was never quite able to bring himself to believe that God had completely abandoned him. He held the conviction that perhaps it pleased God that he had persevered through adversity. And though it did not seem that God had directly intervened to spare the harvest by any miracle, it was God that had joined his life with that of Eve's, and through her, his faith had been restored. For this, Adam felt beholden to God and each day offered a prayer of thanks.

The time of grayness and chill again drew near as Eve's body further effloresced, the fruit of their union growing within her, causing her to become more voluptuous with each passing day. The movements of the unborn child at times seemed restless, and Eve would sit quietly and focus her breath in a slow, rhythmic pattern. Through this, she was often able to calm both herself and the baby, though this same thing had never seemed to placate Cain when he was within her womb, and his erratic movements had often caused her discomfort and pain. Even now that he was older, Eve found she could never quite be certain how he would respond to her attempts at calming him when he became upset. His temper seemed to flare at times without warning, and any small sense of injustice could affect him. These strong reactions often caused Eve great distress, and occasionally even troubled her sleep, though Adam often seemed able to overlook Cain's reactions as insignificant. There were moments when Eve, too, was able to forget these troubling tendencies, for in his great capacity for sensitivity, Cain could be a very sweet child, and he seemed to work hard to gain the approval and affection of his parents.

Despite all of the various differences and similarities between her time of carrying Cain and the carrying of this child, she knew with certainty that there would again be great pain and struggle to bring the baby forth, but found this time that she did not fear it.

Chapter 20

Though she had barely slept during the night, Eve was filled with a lucent energy as she arose to tend to Cain and Adam's morning meal. She herself did not eat, and though it was difficult, she waited for them to finish, and finally when she could no longer contain herself, she let the words burst forth excitedly from her lips.

"Adam, I have felt the readying of my flesh throughout the night! Before this day passes, we shall be blessed!"

Adam's eyes glistened with joy. Cain however, did not understand what his mother meant, and demanded to know what the blessing would be.

"Cain, we have told you many times that there is life within my belly. Today the child will be born and our family will grow. You, too, began in my belly and entered this world small and naked."

Cain remained uncertain and anxious, not completely understanding, and unsure if he wanted another child in his home. He silently took leave of the hut, going out into the bright sunshine to carve rows into the soft dirt where he had cleared away a small patch of grass. He often did this, playing that he was creating his own field to sow and to harvest, just like his father. He pretended his patch of land was much greater than his father's, though, and that it only appeared small because he himself was so big. He always felt calmer when he did this; it made him feel as though it was something he could control.

Inside the hut, Adam and Eve made preparations. Eve felt that most of the day would elapse before the birth, but wanted Adam to stay with her and care for Cain until her time was near.

"Though I feel the tension rise and fall, it is not yet pain. I get comfort from movement and walking, so let us walk to the river and gather fresh water to bring to the hut to have when it is needed. Let us also have the skins prepared to swaddle the babe for warmth. There will be no time for you to do these things after, as Cain will be in need of your attention."

After all had been made ready in the hut, and most of the day's light had passed, Eve felt the tension of her body begin to transform to intervals of pain. Eve knew she wanted to again be at the water when the child came; thus the three of them settled by the bank of the pool and remained there as the westward sky became lit in layers of lavender and pink, then orange and crimson, until finally these colors faded to give way to the indigo of night.

Beneath the still and silent starry sky Eve felt a violent storm ravaging within her. She made great efforts to hide her agony from Cain, who, despite Adam's attempts at occupying him with talk about plants and crops and seeds and other things he was usually so inquisitive about, would not allow himself to be distracted from focusing on his mother. He sought constant reassurance that she was alright. Regardless of his concern, he was too afraid of what was happening to his mother to venture very near to her. He was even briefly relieved when his father moved him farther away from where his mother was, taking him to sit beneath a large silvery birch, until he heard her let out a wailing cry that made his stomach ache and his flesh become sticky and cold with sweat. Adam tried to calm Cain and assure him that it would soon be over and his mother would be fine, though he himself grew more uncertain and anxious as he knew the time of birth was growing closer. Soon he would need to leave Cain alone so he could attend to Eve's labor.

When finally Eve called to Adam, he bid Cain to remain at the tree. Cain watched as his father helped his mother into the water. Under the glow of the pale moonlight he could scarcely make out their shapes nor clearly discern their movements, but he could still hear her. The sound of her shrieking in anguish caused him to tremble and he began weeping. He did not want her to hurt like this and could not understand why his father did not make it stop. He clung to the tree and squeezed his eyes shut, but her cries continued to torment him. He loosened his grip from the birch and held his hands tightly over his ears as he tried to let his own screams drown out the sound of hers.

*   *   *

Cain had continued on like this until he exhausted himself and lost consciousness, sleeping through the remaining hours of the night with his body folded over the wide fork in the trunk of the birch. In the early light of morning, his father roused him and scooped him up in his arms. He carried him to where Eve and their newborn son lie wrapped up in a large animal skin on the grassy edge of the pond. Cain blinked the sleepiness out of his eyes as his head cleared from dreaming. He saw his mother cradling a tiny being who was suckling at her breast, just as he used to. His mother looked tired, but her expression as she gazed down at this small stranger was peaceful and happy. Cain beheld this sight at first with confusion. Then he began to feel a wrenching, sickening pressure in his stomach as realization descended upon him. Hot tears filled his eyes and burned as they rolled down his cheeks.

"No!" he shouted. "It can't stay here!"

Eve held back her dismay and tried to calm his reaction by reaching out to lay her hand upon Cain's head and speaking gently to him.

"Cain, this is your brother. You shall watch over him and protect him. You shall teach him. You shall love him and keep him safe."

"I shall not love him or protect him! I shall not keep him safe! His coming here made you hurt and made you cry! He tried to take you from me! You're *mine*!"

Cain wanted to steal the babe away from his mother's breast, but knew they would be angry with him. Instead he turned to run. "I'll leave them and they'll never see me again, then they'll be sorry," he thought. "Then they'll wish I was still their only son!"

He had scarcely begun to move when his father was suddenly behind him grasping him firmly by the shoulders, stopping him. Neither Adam nor Eve admonished him for his harsh words. Though it caused them both immense sadness, they had known that it was possible that Cain would have great difficulty accepting the new child. There had been signs.

Chapter 21

Although labor had not come easier for her the second time, all of her pain and anguish was dissolved and forgotten the moment she beheld the face of her newborn child. Eve had found an immediate familiarity and a sense of intrinsic recognition between herself and the second son of Adam, unto whom they bestowed the name 'Abel'. And though her heart did not weigh a difference between her love for either child, in her soul she knew that in her arms was a being so much more like herself. She felt that this child's spirit was woven more of the same matter, the same essence, as her own.

Eve felt rapt within a quiet sense of fulfillment when Abel nurtured at her breast. To feed and cradle him satisfied a deep purpose for her. She understood that this was part of the gift of being a mother- to give completely of yourself for the life you created and knowing that in doing so you are receiving abundantly more than what you have given. She had, of course, experienced moments of a similar concordance when she had held Cain at her bosom, though it was often a transient, fluctuating thing. There was something in his countenance that, both now and during his infancy, often made him seem a stranger to her. She longed to close the distance that existed between them, but there was something in him that eluded her, something unknowable, untouchable. It made her heart yearn, but here, with Abel, her heart was replete with the communion they shared between them.

Adam had sensed it too. He often remarked on how kindred Abel's expressions and disposition were to Eve's. He said there seemed a harmony that flowed between them. This connection they shared grew even deeper, as they spent much of their days in each other's quiet company. Adam had decided that in order to diminish the obvious distress Abel's birth had caused Cain that it would be best if he went to the fields with Adam every day, at least until enough time had passed to allow him to acclimate to the change. Cain had always seemed happiest in the fields, and tried to emulate his father, wanting to be big and strong like him, and wanting to be able to make things grow, to have power over the land.

*   *   *

Time passed and both sons grew quickly, seeming to Eve to be taller and stronger each morning than when she had put them to sleep the night before. Cain eventually appeared to accept Abel's presence, and when Abel had learned to walk and speak, Cain even seemed to enjoy teaching him about things. Though he was often boastful of his role as first-born son, Adam and Eve were relieved to see Cain give attention to his brother and had decided that some days he should remain at the hut so that Eve could foster the bond between them. Yet, Eve remained reluctant in allowing her sons to play away from her watchful eye. She had at times seen Cain act in ways that showed little regard for Abel's safety, often leading him into situations that were potentially dangerous. Adam assured her that it was merely his innocence that made him unaware of the dangers that could befall his brother. He said that Cain just didn't understand that because Abel was younger and not yet as strong, that he could not do all of the things Cain could. Though it saddened her and made her feel guilty, Eve was not entirely sure that this was the reason, and so she stayed near whenever the boys were playing or exploring together.

But this was not the only reason she kept watch over their play. She loved to see the delight they took in discovering new things. Through them, she was able to experience the fresh innocence and wonder that she had felt when she was witnessing all of creation for the first time. She envied them their childhood, to be able to learn things in a gradual way, a way that corresponded with the growth of their bodies and minds. She wondered at how their perceptions of the world differed from hers. She realized that though she had not grown from infancy as her sons, she indeed had been as a child in Eden. In many ways, perhaps she still was, as she still derived an innocent sense of awe from experiencing the world through them. They frequently came to her with curiosities and questions that she herself had never considered. Questions about the nature of different herbs, questions about the stars, questions about the seasons, and the clouds and the rains and the rivers, questions about everything they saw. In this way, both of her sons were very much like Eve. They both sought to understand and to know. Though for Cain it was in order to dominate and control his world, and for Abel it was to more fully love and respect all things.

If Cain's place was among the fields, Abel's was among the beasts. Abel would often bring small creatures that had been hurt or abandoned to the hut. He had a gentle way with them and seemed to instinctively know how to care for them. Th birds and other small creatures did not flee from his presence as they did from his family, and many of the docile beasts allowed him to touch them, as the creatures in Eden had allowed Adam and Eve to do. But they had not dared to try it here until now, when Abel, still a young child, had shown them how to approach the gentler beasts and gain their trust.

Near the time of the fourth harvest since Abel's birth, this affinity with the beasts was tested. Though Cain continued to exhibit a deep need to be given attention and praise for all that he did, and seemed to feel slighted whenever Abel earned favor with their parents, he had not exhibited the malevolence or explosive temper they had seen immediately after Abel's birth. And so it was that Eve had been allowing them to play alone outside the hut when she was tending to the hearth or laying down fresh thrushes upon the floor. She and Adam had hoped that giving Cain the opportunity to watch over Abel would help develop kinship and love between the brothers. It had seemed to be the right thing to do, as these brief episodes of unwatched play had so far occurred without incident.

And so it was that there came a day when Eve decided to allow her sons to remain alone near the hut while she went to the river to get fresh water. She wanted so desperately to trust Cain, she felt as if she were testing herself as well, forcing herself to give him an opportunity to prove himself. In truth, the water could wait, or she could simply take her sons with her. This was something she felt she needed to do, so she could be sure she wasn't judging Cain unfairly, so she could know that the things he sometimes said were just words, and that he truly was good and pure of heart.

Though she hurried to the river and back as quickly as she could, it was not fast enough. When she came within sight of the hut and did not see her sons, she called out to them. Cain soon emerged from behind the southern side of the hut, but Abel was not behind him. She had known from the gripping tension in her abdomen that he wouldn't be.

"Tell me where your brother is!" her voice trembled with fear and exasperation.

Cain merely shrugged his shoulders at her in response. Eve ran wildly in the direction Cain seemed to have come from. She did not need to run far before she found him. Her initial feeling of relief suddenly changed to panic when she saw her son was not alone. A feral cub was there beside him. She stared in disbelief as Abel began to gently stroke its fur while the cub nuzzled him in an affectionate way.

Eve knew that the cub's mother could not be far off. She was moving slowly and cautiously toward Abel to retrieve him when her fear was confirmed. She heard the snapping of twigs and looked up to see the great cat emerging from the brush atop a low, nearby hill, and it began treading toward them. As Eve made a move to reach out to Abel, the cat snarled and bore its teeth at her as its tread became a lunge. She stopped, not knowing what to do, watching helplessly as the feline approached Abel and the cub. Abel did not exhibit any fear as he continued laughing at the way the cub's nuzzling and licking was tickling him, even as the mother cat slowly stalked the perimeter around them. Then, to Eve's utter astonishment, the mother simply sniffed at Abel several times, then grasped the cub by the scruff and turned away, disappearing back into the forest.

Eve stumbled forward and fell to her knees, embracing her child tightly as she laughed and cried hysterically at the same time. Abel, not understanding her fear, thought his mother was just being silly. He laughed along with her, having no awareness he had ever been in danger.

When Eve's emotions had calmed somewhat, she gathered Abel up, enfolding him within her arms, and carried him home. Cain was sitting near the doorway of the hut, drawing his pretend rows of crops into the dirt as he still often did. Eve expected him to leap up when he saw them, either from relief or to offer apologies, or both. He did neither. Instead he remained just as he was, and Eve found she could not read his expression. This apathy in him flared her anger so fiercely that she dared not speak to him. She could not trust herself to control her fury at this moment.

She waited until both of her sons had fallen asleep before telling Adam what had happened. Neither of them could comprehend why Cain acted this way, and even worse, Cain did not seem to recognize the depth of his wrongful act. Once more, they decided he would be separated from his brother and go to the fields every day with Adam.

As Eve lie in sleepless reflection she couldn't help but wonder over and over about the Tree. A part of her desperately wished she could take Cain to the Garden and give him Fruit from the Tree of Knowledge so his eyes could be opened and he would Know what is Good and what is Evil. How unfair that it was lost to him, and that God would keep this gift from her son. Perhaps Cain was right in the way he constantly acted as if he were treated unjustly; it was not a just world if he didn't have the opportunity to Eat and to Know.

Had God blessed her with the gift to create this beautiful life, her son, only to deprive the child of the opportunity for Goodness? Eve fell asleep angry with God and with herself. But her heart, as ever, remained open, and where there is openness God speaks, and Eve knew to attend to the insights of her dreams, as she had always found answers and wisdom within them.

She saw herself walking in the Garden. It felt wonderful, like going home. She immediately went to the Tree, wanting to behold its splendor once more, wanting to see how its leaves glistened so brightly in the sun, and to feel the power and energy it emitted. How amazing it would be, she thought, to taste the sweetness of its Fruit once again. In her dream, it appeared just as magnificent as it had so long ago. She approached it and pulled off the ripest piece of Fruit. As soon as she ate it, however, the Tree began to wither and die, dissolving into the earth. It was gone, but had left behind one small, perfect, flowering branch at her feet. She picked it up, and instantly all of Eden, too, began to wither to dust, until there was nothing left of it except for the branch she held in her hand. Her surroundings then suddenly changed, and she saw herself now sitting in the middle of the hut. All the world was silent, and Adam was there, beside her. Without words she extended the branch toward him, and together they planted it in the dirt floor. It grew instantly into a fully matured tree, even more radiant and abundant with sacred Fruit than the Tree from which it was born. And then her sons were there, standing at their feet and reaching up to them with open hands. She and Adam pulled down the best Fruits and gave them to Cain and Abel. As her children ate, she knew that they were able to See and Know, just as when she and Adam had eaten the Fruit. Then, before her eyes, her sons became grown men. They turned and walked out of the hut, out into the world, but she could no longer see them, and was unable to see the path that they had chosen. But they had eaten the Fruit and tasted the wisdom that she and Adam had given them, and their actions would be up to them.

Eve woke up from her dream, no longer angry with God. No longer angry with herself. She now understood that she and Adam possessed the Fruit of Knowledge within themselves and that it was up to them to pass this gift on to their children, and to teach them how to see and how to choose between Good and Evil.

Chapter 22

Time was marked by the seasons of sowing, cultivation, ripening, and reaping of the harvest, followed by the quiet periods of dormancy and decay. This cycle had repeated many times, and Eve had come to bear many sons and daughters.

Cain had grown into a man and had chosen a wife from among his sisters. He established a household of his own and plotted a field of land separate from his father's. Cain farmed the soil through two harvests in the manner he had been taught. His sweat fell upon the earth, his muscles ached, his hands grew calloused, and his patience wore thin in waiting for the fruition of his labors.

Though Cain and Abel had spent most of their younger days apart, as they had grown older they often worked together. Abel had always loved his brother, and did not understand that the separation in their youth had been due to his parents concern for his own safety. He had simply believed it was Cain's great love for the land that caused him to go with their father to the fields each day, never suspecting any other reason. And though Cain still held resentment in the simple fact of Abel's birth, he had come to take comfort in knowing that he was Adam's first son, that it was he who was called to follow the vocation of their father, it was he who now had a wife and a house of his own, and he was sure that not even his brother could take these things from him.

Abel had lessened the strain upon his father and Cain by showing them ways to use the power of the oxen to pull the heavy stones for tilling across the soil, as well as to carry large amounts of water from the river to irrigate the crops. The beasts responded to Abel's gentle ways and were able to be guided to take the yoke upon their backs and go where they were led. The oxen grazed freely among the fields and were only put to work during the early, cooler part of the day: at least in the beginning. Eventually, however, Cain had decided that if he made greater use of the beasts, he could increase his yield with less of his own efforts. He had other ideas as well, and he boasted of them to his brother.

"I'm going to make the plants grow faster and my land will produce more than our father's. He watches and waits too much. I will also increase the breadth of my plot and produce greater bounty, then I will only have to eat the very best of my harvest, and what is not good enough can be discarded. I will shorten the time of dormancy between planting and cause the earth to give up its gifts to me and I shall be endowed with what is mine."

Abel answered, "I have often heard our father say 'you cannot hasten the harvest'. But I do not know the land as you both do, so perhaps you should take your ideas to him and listen to his wisdom and accept his guidance."

Cain was abashed that his younger brother did not look upon him with the respect he felt he deserved, and even more so that Abel would regard him as still being subject to their father's rule. He became determined to prove himself great in Abel's eyes.

"I followed his ways in the field and learned from his skill when I was a child. But now it is my turn to demonstrate my own influence over the land. It is true, you do not understand the soil as I do, so it is a waste to tell you of these things. When I tell our father of my insights, he will recognize the greatness in what I have planned. Then you will not be able to deny it, you will see it too."

Cain yearned deeply for his father's approval, and despite the self-assured boasting he had displayed to his brother, his stomach was knotted with anxiety as he went to Adam, fearing his father would shun his ideas. Indeed, he was right to feel this way. After hearing Cain out, Adam shook his head sadly with disappointment.

"Cain, after all of the days you labored beside me you must understand that the soil and the sun and the seeds work in their own time, they do not bend to the desires of men. You already do wrong in how you treat the oxen, which have served you and made your labors easier. I have seen how you work them in the heat without rest or water or regard for them. You often keep them bound on short tethers, restricting their space for grazing. Now you think to further exert your own will upon the life of this earth without respect for the intrinsic nature of that life. You will cause discordance between yourself and the land if you disregard its cycles and if you take from it more than you have given it.

"I once thought as you do, that nature exists to do my bidding and to benefit me. It is true that man can derive abundance from the earth, but only if he maintains an understanding of the ways of nature. You have a great gift to be able to propagate the grain that makes our bread; you must respect the process and abide by it."

Cain did not want to hear this. He turned from his father and went his own way. He could not allow the vision of his great field to be spoiled. His mother and father had told him how God had given men the charge of the land and the beasts. He would take these things and be master of them.

Chapter 23

Cain had proceeded to increase the expanse of his field and continued to replant it almost immediately after each reaping. He made use of the oxen until they appeared ready to collapse before giving them drink or resting them. He had kept them working in order to ensure his plants were properly irrigated. This was not easy, as the dirt grew dry much faster since he had cleared away most of the brush and trees that had surrounded his field. He thought they would compete with his crops for sun and minerals, and had not understood that their roots helped the land retain moisture. It was now nearing the fourth harvest since he had refused the ways of his father, and his yield had been greater each time. But this season, as he walked the rows of grains he could see that something was very wrong. The color of the stalks appeared dull, not golden and vibrant as they should be. Nor were they growing as tall as before. He had decided to sow the seeds closer together to make use of every portion of soil in his field, and now the stalks were choking each other out. He would have to thin them, putting to waste much of what he had grown.

Cain was as determined as ever to prove that his way would increase his bounty, and he refused to seek his father's advice. But now he had not only a wife, but children of his own that he needed to provide for, so each day he labored from long before the dawn until far past dusk in order to save his crops. His hands blistered and bled worse than they ever had. In his zealous efforts to make up for the soil's lack of water, he gave it too much. Soon after, his misfortune was compounded, as it rained for many days. His crops were flooded and began to rot. His entire field was soon destroyed. He had failed. Cain then did something he hadn't done for many years: he cried.

He slept very little and had not spoken with his parents or siblings for many days. He was too ashamed to tell them of his strife, but they knew. Eve came to him to try to comfort him, and when this did not work she spoke to her daughter, Cain's wife, and counseled her to be patient with Cain and to let him lean on her for support. Eve felt Adam would better understand how to help Cain, for he knew the hardships of laboring in the soil and the despair and hopelessness of a failed crop after investing so much into the land.

When Adam spoke with him, he assured Cain that his family would not go hungry. Adam told him that he could come and work alongside him in his field and he would be free to share in all of his harvest that year. His offer of help did not come free of conditions nor without admonishment.

"You have exhausted the soil. You shall now allow your land to remain fallow for two full years to allow nature to recapture it and replenish it. Then, if it is God's will, it will again be ready for cultivation. During this time, you will also aid your brother in the care of the plow oxen. You will learn from him and hearken to what he says, doing as he bids. Abel has an understanding of life that you do not yet possess. I pray that you grow to be more like him in this way."

Cain's gratitude at his father's kindness was edged with bitterness. He could feel the sourness of bile churning in his belly upon hearing his father speak of Abel with such high esteem, and telling him he must obey his younger brother. He felt stripped of his inherent status as the elder son to be forced into this deference toward Abel. Yet, he would do as his father said, and he would move his family to his father's house, which would not only make it easier for him to assist his father and allow for his family to be taken care of, but it would also spare him of having to look each day upon the ruins of his own failure. In some ways, he even looked forward to the time he would spend with Adam. It would be like when he was young, working in his father's field, and perhaps he truly could start over.

But it was more difficult for him than he had anticipated to feel so completely dependent upon his family after having established a house of his own. He felt subjugated and lowered in every way. Day after day he witnessed how his family looked upon Abel with a deep love and regard. It seemed as if Abel, not Cain, had been blessed by God to be the favored son. He saw that not only his mother and father, but his younger brothers and sisters, and even his own children, delighted in the way Abel would show them how to gain the trust of the animals, how to care for them and even play with them. Abel had even brought some of the smaller creatures inside the hut, allowing them to sleep next to the children at night with them. Cain could scarcely tolerate this.

But even worse than these things, Cain felt further divested of his birthright in having to follow his brother in leading the oxen to the river at the end of each day to water and rest them from their labors. Cain did not think it was right that he be made to feel as if he served the animals. He felt it was menial work for a man who tilled the soil to also have to care for the beasts. On their way back from the river one evening, Cain voiced his feelings of distaste for this chore to Abel.

Abel responded, "Brother, the better you serve them, the better they will serve you. That is the way with all things. Did you not learn this from your trials in the field? You did not respect the ways of nature, and that is why you lost your crops. It is for your benefit that these beasts have labored, and so you should be grateful to them. I pray that you may one day understand these truths."

Cain's emotions flared at the mention of his miseries and at hearing his brother talk to him as if he had some greater authority or wisdom. Of all of the hardship and disgrace Cain had to bear, this innocent remark from his brother was suddenly too much for him. His senses were lost to him as his weakened spirit became overwhelmed by the rush of rage and fury. Before he realized what he was doing, he grabbed a heavy river stone that lay upon their path, raised it up high and brought it down with heavy force, striking the base of Abel's skull with a sickening 'thunk'. Abel folded and fell.

Cain stood motionless, staring at the body of his brother lying dead upon the dirt. For several moments he did not breathe or blink, and his own heart seemed to have stopped beating

"This cannot be real," he thought. But it was. He hurled the blood-stained stone far into the trees, then turned away from his brother and began to vomit violently.

When he had stopped, he held his eyes tightly shut, imagining that when he turned around he would open them to see Abel getting up from the ground. Instead, when he finally gathered enough courage to look, all he saw was his brother's body exactly where it had fallen, limp and lifeless, next to the growing stain of the dark viscid pool spreading upon the ground.

Cain fell to his knees and wrapped his arms around his brother, cradling him. It was the only time he could recall ever having touched him. He suddenly had a vision of Abel as an infant. "I should have held you then!" he cried out. "I should have loved you and protected you! I am so wretched! God has truly cursed me to be so spiteful and vile!"

"I take it back!" he screamed to Heaven. "I revoke this act and wish death instead upon myself! I beg of You, let it be me! My brother's heart was pure and mine was filled with envy and malevolence, yet I still breathe while my sweet and innocent brother lies dead."

Cain had to let go of Abel's body and move away from it to be sick once more.

Chapter 24

Eve had been awaiting the return of her two eldest sons from the river. The sun had nearly set and they had been longer than usual in coming home. She tried to ignore the unsettling, intuitive tension in her belly.

When at last she saw Cain come walking from the river with his brother cradled limply in his arms, Eve needed no words from his lips to understand what had happened. She could see the guilt in the way he walked, even from a distance. She gripped at her abdomen and wailed a long doleful cry as she realized that a part of her had feared this very thing all of Cain's life. He approached her and gently laid Abel's body at her feet.

Eve fell upon Abel, and the rest of the world disappeared. She could see nothing through the blur of her red and swollen eyes. She could hear nothing but her own laments filling the air. She could smell nothing but the mixed scent of animals and earth that Abel always had about him. She could taste nothing but the salt of the tears that fell down her face and onto her lips. She could feel nothing but the still and vacant bones and flesh of what used to be her beloved Abel. Then, she did not even perceive these things, as she collapsed beside his body and the world went black.

Each moment of the days that followed was something to be endured; to be survived. She had not known that the breadth and width of her heart was so vast that it could contain this much despair and agony. During the day she composed herself for the sake of her children, allowing them to grieve and be comforted by her. But at night, when she thought everyone was asleep, she would light a torch and go out into the darkness, away from her family so she could mourn alone by the river where he died. There she let the memories of Abel's childhood wash over her. These memories would never again be clean. They would forever be tinged with the pain of his death. Whenever she recalled watching him laugh and play it would not only bring a smile to her lips, but also tears to her eyes and a tightening in her throat. She could feel her loss and sadness like a blade that cut at her abdomen, as if cutting her womb, within the place where Abel's life had begun. It was a terrible thing to be so full of pain, yet feel so barren and empty at the same time.

Eve had wanted to wash and prepare her son's body to express her love for him in a tangible way. She needed to caress her sweet boy and anoint him with water and oil. She needed to adorn him with the most fragrant of flowers and clothe him in new, clean raiment. And so, for three days Eve and her daughters tended to Abel's body.

Despite her sadness, she found that she could love Cain no less. He was the only one whose suffering was as profound as her own. A part of her longed to cradle Cain in her arms and give him solace from his pain. She knew his grief and shame would remain as a curse upon him, marking him with torment until the day of his own death. She wanted to keep him close to her to protect him from hurting, but she could not. She knew she could not bear to look upon his face day after day, for his face was one of the last things Abel had beheld before his eyes had closed forever.

Cain had not run away in his shame. He stayed and endured the looks of scorn and hatred his brothers and sisters cast upon him. With the exception of his wife, they shunned him and would not speak to him. He slept alone in his own hut these nights, feeling he deserved to dwell within the wasteland and misery of his ruined field. He had remained only for the purpose of assisting his father with the building of a cairn, where Abel would be buried on the third day. He stayed until the last stone was laid upon the mound, and then Cain, along with his wife and children, prepared to leave.

Adam helped his son by giving him many of his best farming tools, as well as a stock of new seeds to plant. He had hitched a cart onto two of the oxen for carrying Cain's belongings, as well as the children when they tired of their journey. Cain felt a knot in his stomach when he saw that his father meant for him to take the animals.

"I promise I will care for the beasts just as Abel would have. In all that I do, I will act as my brother. I promise I will respect all things in life as he did. I promise.... I promise....," His words broke off as he began to weep.

Adam said to him, "Life will not be easy for you, and your burdens will be many. If you persevere through all of your trials and stay true to these promises you have made, you will, indeed, honor your brother. Abel always loved you and I believe he still would love you today. I love you, too. Do not doubt that." After they had finished loading the cart, Eve approached to say her final words to him. Adam left them so mother and son could be alone.

Eve had not looked upon him since it had happened, and she knew she would never look at her eldest son again after this day. But now, for one last time, she gazed intently into Cain's eyes. Beneath his sorrow she saw something there that had eluded her throughout his entire life. She saw his soul. It was the soul of a man who was no longer a stranger to her. It was the soul of her son, and she knew it was Good.

"Your grief over the loss of your brother has opened your eyes. It was a bitter and rancid Fruit that you have tasted in order for you to undergo this revelation. How can I be glad for it? I am torn by this conflict. Cain, whom I have loved and nurtured at my breast, I mourn losing you, even as it is now, with this new wisdom you have gained that you have been born anew and shall truly be free to live the rest of your life. Your act has taken two sons from me, for it is time for you to leave this place. I fear that it is too full of heartache here for you to bear. I also fear that even if you wished to stay, your brothers may not be able to overcome their hatred for what you have done, and would not understand if your father and I allowed you to remain. They may seek to harm you, and this I could not abide."

Eve held Cain's face tenderly in her hands as she continued, "Ever shall you be my first-born son, and I will pray for your heart to remain open and for all of your actions to be pure and one with God. Now go and make a life that is good for your wife and children. Let your children learn wisdom at your knee so they may be spared the torment you have known."

Eve kissed him and embraced him. She struggled desperately against her own arms, which seemed to exert their own will to keep her son protectively within them. But at last she released him and let him go. She tried to turn away, but she could not. She stood transfixed and watched as Cain joined his family and they walked further and further away from her until they had disappeared completely and forever from her sight. Even then, she could not leave. She felt his departure wasn't final until she left the place of their 'goodbye'. As long as she remained, she was still somehow part of the moment.

She had fallen asleep in that spot, exhausted from crying. Adam came to check on her just before nightfall. He gathered her up in his arms and carried her home. She did not wake up until the next morning. There was a hushed, hesitant quality all around her, and her children spoke very little. Their feelings were conflicted. For the most part they were still in shock that such a thing could have truly happened. They missed Abel terribly, and in differing degrees felt sad for Cain in turns, and despised him in turns. They felt sadness, too, for their mother and father.

Chapter 25

For countless nights Eve would steal away so she could weep freely and mourn in solitude. With no one near to hear her, she would cry out loud as her hands raked and tore at her breast, praying to somehow rid herself completely of her heart and the burning, acidic agony it brought to torment her. She despised it for having the capacity to keep beating amid her pain and loss. It felt as if each time it pulsed, it circulated its pain throughout the rest of her body. She didn't want to be strong enough to endure this misery.

Then came a time when she was too worn for crying, too worn for most anything. These torpid days of grey lethargy seemed to stretch on interminably before her. Inertia, however, is not the natural state of things, least of all of the spirit or the heart, and Eve's emotions continued to evolve with the passage of time. Just as despair and lament had given way to apathy, listlessness became replaced by days that were marked by the fluctuating rise and fall of her emotions. Resentment, guilt, and anger, all in turn, were visited upon her.

She resented the sun for rising each day and continuing to bathe the world in its warmth and light as if nothing had changed. How dare it shine so brightly in the clear blue sky as if her sons had not been taken from her? So too did she resent the gentle winds, the blossoming flowers, the cool rushing river, the starlit heavens, and everything else that had ever given her joy. But more than anything, she cursed herself, for with the passing of time she began to find moments of happiness in these little things once again. She would catch herself humming along with the songs of the birds, or would feel a sense of a sweet lightness as she breathed in a fragrant breeze. She would then become laden with anger and guilt at realizing that she could, even for a moment, abandon her sorrow and allow her thoughts to stray from her lost sons. At first she responded by embracing her pain more tightly, determined to dedicate herself to the memories of Abel and Cain.

Adam saw how deeply Eve suffered beneath this flux of emotion. Though his own grief was profound, he did not struggle with all of the conflicts within his pain as she did. He sought to comfort her, to somehow fill the lonely space that Cain and

Abel had left behind. Eve did not make this an easy undertaking, as she often kept herself isolated from him. Since the time of Abel's death and Cain's departure, she had remained a source of strength for her children, allowing them to take refuge in her nurturing love for them, showing patience and acceptance of all of their troubles and cares. Yet, she had not wanted to lay down her own yoke of sadness upon another. She withdrew from Adam, thinking to protect him from bearing the weight of her burdens, not seeing how this barrier she created was causing him distress.

Adam wanted so desperately to ease her suffering and free her from her own resistance to allow herself any joy without the feelings of guilt and penitence that followed. He felt lost and powerless as he looked upon the woman he loved lying asleep next to him, unable to give her the peace in her waking hours that he hoped she was at least allowed in slumber.

Because of this Adam was unable to sleep, so troubled was he by her grief. He went out and sat beneath the starlit sky upon the heather and clover just outside their door. Lulled by its sweet gentle scent mixed with the evening dew, he lay down upon the soft ground and his thoughts drifted to the pleasant memories this fragrance aroused in him. Suddenly he recalled the time when he and Eve had made love on this same patch of earth so many years ago, when this scent of heather had mixed with Eve's own lovely essence. He remembered how he had felt so lost in despair over the drought of that year. Eve had brought his spirit back to life and rekindled his desire not only for her, but his desire for life and for joy. He wanted to give her what she had given to him, not only then, but in all their days together. He realized that Eve herself had shown him the answer, and now he would do the same for her.

Adam plucked a handful of the flowers and brought them into the hut, laying them beside Eve so she would smell them as she breathed in. Within a few breaths the fragrance roused her to the sweet hazy state between being fully asleep and fully awake. She smiled and sighed with pleasure at their influence on her senses. She responded to Adam's touch upon her skin and to his kisses on her mouth. With her mind not yet alert enough to interfere with the natural impulses of her body and her spirit, she gave herself over fully to the sensual abandon of the moment, and her breath quickened with the excitement of their connection as Adam made love to her.

Once the sublime moment had reached its crescendo, Eve's cries of passion changed to sobs. Love had caused her to relax and yield, removing the defensive shield that had become encompassed within the tension of her flesh. Her heart could no longer hold onto her sadness. And when she had finally let go, all of her barriers dissolved away and were released through her tears.

Eve continued to weep, and Adam kept her wrapped within his arms, wanting her to be able to absorb the comfort of his strength and to fill her emptiness with the energy of his devotion. She lifted her head from Adam's chest to look at him as she spoke.

"I was wrong to keep my sadness restrained in your presence. On this night, as with every time you touch me or enter into me, my soul reveals itself and my heart surrenders to this love. Our spirits are so intimately known to each other that they are woven together as one, and I cannot turn you out from my heart, for you are my heart, just as I am yours."

Chapter 26

Within the year, Eve was blessed with the birth of another son, whom they named Seth. Though it would be impossible to fill the vacant space in her life left by the absence of Cain and Abel, Seth brought her great joy, and he grew to be a righteous and good man.

Seth was not the last of the children to be born to Adam and Eve, and their descendants flourished and spread throughout the lands, establishing their own houses. They became fishers, farmers, hunters, or builders for their sustenance. They traded among each other and benefited from the skills of their brothers. Eve was delighted when those who had journeyed afar would return to tell of the different animals and plants they had seen, and of the great mountains, rivers, seas, and forests they had discovered. Their descriptions told her that it was just as she had hoped, and that many of the creatures that she and Adam had known in Eden did indeed dwell elsewhere upon the earth.

The story of the Garden, their exodus, and of the curses was passed down to each generation, and Eve and Adam witnessed how differently their children, and their children's children, responded to what they heard. The same words could inspire one child to seek out the Good in everything around them, while another might become infatuated with the idea of searching for Eden, hoping to discover a life of perfection, free from their everyday cares, not understanding the lessons of their parents.

Eve tried to bestow the wisdom unto her daughters that would guide them to live their lives in such a way that would lessen the impact of the curses that could befall them as women. Though she herself had no mother nor sister to go before her and teach her of these things, she explained as best she could, from her own experience the sacred mysteries of the female flesh as it ripens into that of a woman and becomes ready to create and nurture life. She did not want her daughters to fear or detest this, but to recognize, respect, and honor the strength and beauty of their femininity. Woman would not have been burdened with that which she did not possess the ability to transcend.

Eve wanted her daughters to understand that all children are as the fertile ground, born with the seed of Knowledge, lying as an uncultivated potential within them. As her daughters reached the age of childbearing, she would tell them:

"As mothers, women have been given the gift of growing the fruit of this seed within their children. You must make your own life an example for them, lest you be further cursed to witness the ignorance of your children and be deprived of seeing them grow strong and wise. As you behold the lives of your children, you will feel both their joys and their sorrows in your heart as if they are your own joys and sorrows. When it befell women to bear children in pain, it was not merely woes of physical pain, but the desperate longing for our children to be kept safe and free from suffering that became our yoke to bear. I learned this lesson deeply when my own sweet Cain was unable to see with the Knowledge of Good and Evil, blinded and weakened by envy. I had taught him the same lessons that I had taught to Abel, yet their choices and their understanding of Good and Evil were not the same. Cain was lost, and he was guilty of many things, but he was not evil. It was when his judgment had been cast in shadow that he could not see the path that his true nature could have illuminated for him. And even with the seed of Knowledge that Adam and I tried to nurture within him, Cain's life could not change until he chose to open his eyes and allow the Goodness of his true nature into his heart.

"Just as Cain, your children, too, may turn away from Truth and Goodness. And when you see them stumble and fall in their choices and when you witness their pain, you may nurture and love them, but their souls and their choices will remain their own. You cannot impose your will upon them.

"I have felt empathy with God in seeing the struggles of my children. A mother longs to give her children everything, just as all was provided for Adam and myself in the Garden. But this results in dependence and ingratitude, and divests a person of the opportunity of developing a sense of autonomy and accomplishment, and from knowing true freedom. When they are ready, you must open the gates for your children to let them flourish on their own, just as the gates of Eden were opened to release us. It was difficult and painful, yet necessary for our own growth.

"A woman must also take care to lessen the curse of what she must bear in her life when she chooses a husband. It has been proclaimed that a woman shall suffer her passion and her longing to give and receive love. It would seem that this is so, for have seen those among my daughters who have truly been cursed with the misery of an unwise choice. When a woman chooses a man who is weaker than she, so she can rule over him, she cannot respect him and soon becomes frigid and bitter towards him. In seeking this control and dominance over a man, she loses her feminine beauty, which is her true strength. There can be no love or happiness there, and he may seek fulfillment from another, and their agonies and deceptions will be multiplied. And when a woman desires a man who is not good to her, who berates and mistreats her, she damns herself to suffering. It degrades a woman to consummate with a man unworthy of her, who robs her of her dignity and subjugates her to his will. Sadly, it seems that in the absence of love to unify man and woman, the woman may respond by clinging more tightly to try to maintain the connection to one who does not befit her, and she loses herself in the effort of this grasping. To endure a wretched marriage does not serve any beneficial end. Suffering only begets suffering.

"However, if a woman gives herself to one who fulfills her desires, who recognizes and cherishes her unique beauty, and who is strong in his own right, his love will fortify her, and she will receive back all that she has given." Eve told her daughters of the dream she had had years earlier that showed her the nature of how love is reciprocated between man and woman when each strengthens the other by their unique male and female energies, combining to become perfect in their union. "To settle for anything less than this deprives both lovers from ascending to their highest state of bliss. To experience the ecstasy of a pure, untainted communion with another opens us to communion with the essence of God. *Who* we love and *how* we love are reflections of what is valued within our hearts and minds, and love begets love."

Just as Eve had tried to impart her wisdom unto her daughters, so too, did Adam undertake to teach his sons the lessons he had learned. He wanted to spare them what Cain had endured and lessen the tribulations in their lives.

"As a man walks upon the earth, he has choices which lie before him at all turns. A man may harness the energy and the elements of this earth to create sustenance and joy for himself and his family, and in so doing he also creates *himself*, becoming the man he was meant to be. There is some calling or purpose to which each person is beckoned, yet not all will hearken or answer. We are all born as expressions of God and it is through this life that we have been given that the potential of undirected energy becomes focused and purposeful, and we become co-creators with God. Those who deny their calling will walk through life without a sense of meaning in what they do, finding hopeless dread upon waking to each day, always searching for what they do not possess and coveting the lives of their brothers. And there will be those among men who, like Cain, will work against nature, trying to control and manipulate what has been determined since the creation of the universe. For, within the tiniest of seeds already exists the potential for the entire cycle of its life, and man cannot change the course of the seasons, the rising of the sun, or the passing of time. Though he may seem to conquer these forces in small ways for a time, when he acts in ways to try to alter the intrinsic order of life, balance is disrupted and entropy ensues to destroy what he has achieved. Cain will live out his days in penance for his acts against another man and against the soil. If you learn not from my words, heed the lesson of your brother.

"It does not matter if a man harvests grains from the land, draws fish from the waters, gathers trees and stones to build, or hearkens to any other calling that beckons him, all must be mindful and understand that man is a force upon the earth and capable of either perpetuating or laying to waste the bounty before him. The expression of a man's soul can be witnessed in that which he creates."

"Of the lessons I give to you, you must heed this above all: do not commit the error of defining God by your own image. God manifests in our lives in accordance with our expectations. When I was young and rigid in my thinking, I sought canons and limitations to guide my faith, and indeed, it was limitations which I received. God does not demand sacrifice of us, only that we try to live true to the light that dwells within each of us. Do not take it upon yourself to pass judgment on the faith of another, for each man's soul has its own divine relation with God that is sacred and unique."

*   *   *

And thus, Adam and Eve tried to fulfill the commitment vested within them as mother and father to pass on their wisdom to their children, not only by their words, but through embodying their Knowledge of Good, and living as an example for their children to witness. This became more difficult as their descendants continued to multiply and emigrate farther and farther away, filling the lands with their progeny. Though most of their children tried to live in Truth and Goodness, there were those who did not seem to fully comprehend the nature of God, and many Truths came to lose their meaning, becoming entangled within ritual, creeds, and doctrines, despite the cautionary words of Adam.

And as it was passed down through generations, even the story of Adam and Eve, and of Creation, often became distorted and convoluted with ideas of devils and demons which could influence man and keep him from choosing rightfully. Many of their descendents were unable to see that the only demons are those of man's own devising.

*   *   *

Days passed, turning to years, and the flesh of Adam and Eve began to succumb to the effects of their long lives upon the earth. The sun, the wind, gravity, and time had all left their marks upon their skin, and their muscles no longer carried them through their days with the lithe ease they had once known. Weariness came more quickly to their bodies, though in their hearts and minds they continued to feel an unbounded exuberance for life's many wonders, and their love for Creation and for each other remained vibrant and inexhaustible.

Adam had a growing sense of the coming of his death, and one night he called to Eve, asking her to come lie with him among the grove of cypress trees that grew beside his field. As they bedded down upon the earth Adam held Eve, willing his arms to hold her as firmly as he could, imparting the comfort of his strength unto her one last time. There were many things he wished to tell her before he became forever silent. Things she may have already known, yet he wanted to have spoken them to her

"Eve, I know that it continues to worry your heart that our children may have inherited the burden of curses within their lives. Understand that this is false and could never be. We have taught our children that all men have free choice in their actions and no soul can be held accountable for the acts committed by another. Though they may inherit the conditions under which all men must struggle to overcome, all souls are born clean and unmarred by the choices of their ancestors, and all shall be judged only by their own virtue. The curses are merely the natural consequence of not living in accord with creation, and it is in this that a man shall suffer.

"Even for us, who believed ourselves proclaimed cursed for eating the Fruit, when we sought to live our lives in what we recognized as Good, we witnessed how our lives became blessed despite our struggles. And when I reflect upon my days, those burdens are but a wisp of a memory. It is the joys I have known that endure in my heart. It was by our choices that our fate was determined.

"As I speak to you of choices, I have something to say to you that may be difficult for you to accept. It is something I have long wondered about, but with the clarity I have been given as I near the end of this life, I now know with certainty that the power of the Tree was apocryphal, only a myth."

These words indeed caught Eve by surprise and she was momentarily taken aback.

"But…but… how can you say that, when all things changed after we ate it?"

"No," Adam said, "all things changed the moment that I *chose* to eat it with you. When you came to me and told me of your resolve to taste the Fruit, and I spent that long night imagining my life without you, *that* was when I came to recognize the exquisite beauty in your nakedness. That was when I realized I loved you. It was from that love that I received the gift of Knowledge of Good and Evil. To follow you was Good, but to forsake you would have been the greatest Evil I could have committed, for I would have been turning away not only from you, but from my own virtue. In truth, I would have not only been turning away from what is Good, but from what is God."

"But what about the way my eyes were opened when we ate it?" Eve asked.

Adam smiled at this, shaking his head, "Don't you realize that your eyes were always open to seeing the Good all around you. You didn't change at all. Your eyes saw the Truth of my Goodness because I came back to you. You saw that I acted with courage to eat the Fruit, and then you trusted in me. That was the moment you fell in love with me, the moment *before* you ate it.

"I am further convinced of this when I think back upon how you were not drawn to the Tree until you thought it was unique. You sat beneath it all the while that I was talking to you, and never considered it more beautiful than any other. You only saw it as magnificent and felt drawn to it when you thought it held Knowledge.

It was your openness to Knowing that marked you as wise. Without the desire and willingness to see and understand, words are just words, and *Fruit* is just fruit. Had we thought this revelation was to be found in a drink of water, so it would be. If we thought it could be attained through the counting of the stars, so it would be. If we had thought to find it in each other's embrace, so it would be, and, my dearest love, so it was.

"When I implored God to give to me a woman, all I had thought to receive was a companion of flesh, formed as my own from the clay of the earth and with the blood of my marrow. What I received was the very fire and light of the heavens, the power and strength of the rushing rivers, the gentle caress of the wind. What I was given was *you*. God has designed you beautifully, but you, Eve, have created your own Radiance.

"Let me now draw the taste of honey from your kiss once more." Eve's lips met with Adam's and she kissed him long and sweetly. They lay together beneath the open sky throughout the night. Eve slept with her head upon Adam's chest as she had so many times in her life, but never would again.

*   *   *

When she awoke she knelt beside the body and gazed upon. How strange it made her feel to behold what had been "Adam", but was now merely flesh devoid of the spark of life or any of the qualities that had made him who he was. And though his spirit no longer lived in this body, Eve continued to feel his presence as a part of her own life, and she knew with absolute certainty that Adam's love for her had not been altered by death, continuing on infinitely.

She grasped a handful of dirt from this field where Adam had anointed the earth day after day with the sweat and blood of his labors, and she clenched it tightly at her breast. This soil was part of him. His body and spirit had grown strong from it. He had found joy, purpose and pride in working with the earth to create food for those he loved. And now, his body would truly become one with it.

Eve went to Seth and his sons to ask them to inhume Adam's body, returning his flesh unto the dust from which it was created, burying him along the edge of his field. She knew that this is what he would have wanted.

Chapter 27

After Adam's passing, Eve grew ever more reflective. Knowing her own life would soon end as Adam's had, she began to spend much of her time contemplating the meaning and purpose of life if it ultimately leads only to dying.

Abel's death had been sudden, unnatural and lurid. It was a death forced by the actions of another and had caused her to know terrible sorrow and heartache. But Adam's dying seemed the natural completion of something. Though at times she missed seeing his face, hearing his voice, and feeling his presence beside her, she continued to feel his love just as strongly as ever. She took comfort in knowing Adam had been at peace in his last moments, ready for his passage from this life.

Through Adam's example and his work with the soil, Eve had come to understand that man must abide by the intrinsic order of things and follow the natural cycles of birth, growth, maturity, death, and decay. Acceptance of this was necessary for the readying of the ground in order to allow for the birth of something new. This is the way of all things, for, as Adam had once explained to her, even among the heavens, entire star systems burn out, dying away to open up space for new stars to come into existence. No space in the entirety of the universe ever remains vacant or dormant.

She believed that through the death of this physical body, man's soul returns fully to God. And that when the fears, the ego, and the burdens that accompany this human flesh are stripped away we are able to gain the freedom and openness that can allow us to reconnect with the Source from which our lives emanate.

"But need we ever feel so separated from this?" she wondered. She had experienced many moments throughout her life when she knew there was no distinction between herself and the essence of God. Often she had felt this within her dreams, yet this sense of a Divine Union had also existed in the birth of each of her children, within the intimate communion of her body with Adam's, and also within the moments when she would become so completely absorbed in experiencing some aspect of nature that she felt as though she were one with it.

It was within her most intensely sensual and human experiences that she was brought to dwell within a sense of being one with God.

"That may be the purpose of life in this flesh", she thought, "to be a means through which we can experience a tangible communion with our Creator, and to become the manifest form of God's energy and love though our intentions and acts."

Eve had come to realize that her earlier experience of God had often been limited by what she had *perceived* God to be, and she had been restricted in her capacity for understanding this at different times in her life. Yet, because she was open and receptive to them, Eve had frequently experienced those glimpses of the Sacred Truths. She remembered how she had once lamented upon coming to this land from Eden how it seemed as though God had divested her of each of the things in life that had brought her joy. Now, she could see with the wisdom and perspective that time brings, that the opposite was true. With each time of pain and sorrow in her life, she had always come to be blessed in some way. She knew that all she had experienced had been integral, perhaps even necessary, for the evolution of her soul. And as she had evolved, so too had her understanding of God evolved.

For Eve, God was not static, but rather a dynamic, fluent force that continually moves all of life toward balance and harmony. God is ever-expansive and infinite, as is all of Creation, and thus, as was she and as would all of her descendants be, whether they understood and accepted this or not. God is the thread that is woven to connect all things throughout Heaven and Earth.

Eve also understood that God is never absent, and man can never be utterly forsaken. Though man may come to experience hardship or sickness, and conflict may arise between brothers or nations for what they perceive as God's favor, man is never without resources to resolve and heal all that may befall him. In hardship, there is opportunity to co-create with God to forge the strength and fortitude to persevere as long as man does not give up his devotion to what is Good. In sickness, all has been provided within the bounty of Creation to heal and nurture man, but only if man acts with reverence toward these gifts and does not molest or destroy them. And amid conflict, when a man acts against his brethren, blinded to the revelation that God resides within all men, and severs his natural state of unity with God, *even then,* as Eve had witnessed with Cain, a man can return from the darkness and find redemption if his heart opens to the essence of Godliness within him.

It was within the solace of knowing these things that Eve embraced the last of her human experiences. The time had come to allow her flesh to dissolve back to the dust of the earth, and to surrender the light within her to be reflected back unto its Source. Just as Adam, she did not fear what was to come. She knew that it was only her flesh that was ephemeral and transient. Her spirit was eternal, immune to decay and beyond the influence of entropy. Eve could not help but smile at the realization of this final Truth.

Her smile suddenly left her as she choked and gasped violently to draw in one final breath while her lungs expanded and burned painfully with the effort. Eve then released this breath, relinquishing it to become one with the wind and the ether. The next moment there was stillness, lightness, a gentle hush. . .

For my sweet Gabrielle:
You were born perfect and beautiful,
but have created your own radiance.

and to Jill, who is so frequently
my supportive cornerstone.

About the Author:

Janelle Jacobson was born in a small town in southern MN, where she was raised in a conservative Catholic environment. Throughout her years of attending Catholic school she often questioned the church and the "whys" of the dogmatic and restrictive teachings. This tendency inspired the spiritual and self-exploration that resulted in this, her first novel.

Janelle currently lives in St. Paul where she can be close to her most influential inspiration, her daughter.

Made in the USA
Charleston, SC
10 May 2012